BELLE

Other Series by H.P. Mallory

Paranormal Women's Fiction Series:
Haven Hollow
Midlife Spirits
Midlife Mermaid

Paranormal Shifter Series:
Arctic Wolves

Paranormal Romance Series:
Underworld
Lily Harper
Dulcie O'Neil
Lucy Westenra

Paranormal Adventure Series:
Dungeon Raider
Chasing Demons

Detective SciFi Romance Series:
The Alaskan Detective

Academy Romance Series:
Ever Dark Academy

Reverse Harem Series:
Happily Never After
My Five Kings

BELLE

Book 9 of The Happily Never After Series

By

HP Mallory

10 Chosen Ones:
When a pall is cast upon the land,
Despair not, mortals,
For come forth heroes ten.
One in oceans deep,
One the flame shall keep,
One a fae,
One a cheat,
One shall poison grow,
One for death,
One for chaos,
One for control,
One shall pay a magic toll.

Belle:

Distant wrongdoing demands a toll
And a sorceress will pay the fine
And rising from contrition
Shall stop the march of time.

Chapter One
Belle

"We had our asses handed to us!"

Gasping when we stop for a moment to catch our breath, it's the first time I've a chance to comment since our escape. Our poor bodies are as badly battered as our dignity at this point, so my point is a complete understatement.

There are no more than a dozen of us left, the majority of the people we took into Delerood perished within moments of making entry into the city and those who made it out were cornered by Vita, who made quick work of sucking the youth from them, leaving them as elderly shells on the cusp of death. They'd been unable to make it very far before succumbing to a number of ailments they should not have experienced for years to come.

"Well, in hindsight," Pene gasps, "maybe going after Kronos wasn't such a good idea."

Looking over at her, my face falls. Thankfully, she managed to escape the rapid aging curse, but suffered a large gash in her side from an enemy's blade. Blood is pumping past her hand, which she firmly presses over it. How is she even moving, never mind, talking?

Unfortunately, I lost the small bag of healing potions I was carrying on our retreat from Delerood, so I'll have to work with whatever I can find. I gesture at Brennan and say, "Could you help me?"

Brennan and I spend the next few minutes trying to restrict the blood flow from Pene's wound. The best we can do is to pack the puncture with a few bits of spare cloth and lay her down on a blanket to rest. Although she lost a lot of blood, I believe I can still heal the wound. But first, I need to forage for specific herbs and roots to grind into a poultice.

"Anyone else suffering from injuries that require magic?" I ask the others. When no one speaks up, I exhale a sigh of relief and then briefly scan the place where we stopped. Looks safe enough, at least, for the moment, so I yell to everyone, "We'll camp here for now."

"Here?" Brennan asks doubtfully. "We're hardly out of Delerood."

"No one will be coming after us," I answer, shaking my head. "The time loop Kronos placed on the city cuts everyone off from entering or exiting. He can't even use the tides, and I'm sure he'll keep it that way until the final battle. He's too busy buying more time to make further preparations than to bother about us. I'm sure we pose no immediate concern."

Brennan doesn't look convinced. "What kind of preparations does Kronos need to make? Based on what I just saw, he wouldn't face too much adversity if he wanted to finish the job Morningstar started."

"Don't give up so easily," I reply with a tone of reproach. "We've got a long fight ahead of us. Focusing on every little setback won't get us any closer to victory."

"Well, you see a much brighter side than I do."

I suppose that's true. Brennan is a good man and a better soldier and he's quite unacquainted with a sweeping defeat. Truth is: when we entered Delerood, we were already grossly outnumbered. But it's important to remember the righteousness of a cause has nothing to do with the force of its arms. I expect our numbers will change once Bowie finishes retrieving all the souls she inadvertently sent to the ether. By the time we meet Morningstar and his ilk again, we should have all of our soldiers back in the fray.

"Well, seeing how cynical you are, someone's got to provide the optimism," I say before facing Pene again. "I'll be back soon," I tell her, gently patting her cheek.

"No doubt in my mind," she whispers back. She seems a little hazy, which is reasonable after all the blood she's lost.

When I head off into the woods, Brennan follows me. I turn around to face him and shake my head. "I don't need a bodyguard, Brennan."

"I understand that."

"Then?"

"I came to ask what your plan is for our next battle?"

"I don't even know when our next battle will begin," I scoff. I must restrain my irritation lest it interfere with my herb-finding mission. "We narrowly survived this one."

"Such comforting thoughts," he grumbles.

Reluctantly, I interrupt my search because I need to settle whatever this is right now. I stop my foraging and look him fully in the face. "Say what's on your mind, Brennan. No need to mince words."

"Fine," he says with narrowed eyes. "I'll tell you what's on my mind, although I don't think it's going to come as much of a surprise: we're outmatched and outnumbered."

"Both statements will be obsolete when Bowie reanimates all our dead soldiers and they're back on the front lines."

"And when do you think that's going to happen? Not to mention, what might we encounter before it does?" He shakes his head. "Belle, we lost most of our soldiers back there."

"I realize that, Brennan," I agree. "And that's why I'm trying to save one of our warriors now."

"You know what I mean," Brennan insists, displaying his usual impatience. "My point is: right

4

now, we're not fit for *any* battle."

"No one knows that better than me, but it doesn't change the fact that you'll have to give me more time to figure out our next move."

"Just don't *waste* our time," he finishes, turning to march back toward the camp. "Or none of us will be coming home."

I watch his back solemnly for a few moments before returning to the woods. My trained eye uncovers the various flowers, mushrooms and roots I need to grind into a balm for Pene's treatment. I was careful not to tell her how serious her wound was, to avoid frightening her, but the situation is grim. She needs a blood transfusion badly, but we're ill-prepared to do so out here, in the middle of the forest. The ingredients I seek will allow me to restore most of her blood and, hopefully, take away some of her pain.

As bad as our circumstances are now, the peace of the forest welcomes me. It's a long-awaited respite after the chaos in Delerood. How I wish I could just take my time and enjoy this moment, but I don't have that luxury.

Regardless, I can't let Pene die. Her entire family was slaughtered by Kronos—it's the sole reason she's one of my best soldiers—her vendetta against Kronos is personal. After losing so much already, how unjust would it be to let Kronos take her life, too? It's a question I'm not prepared to answer.

I shake my head as I gather my ingredients. Brennan's ominous predictions keep returning to my thoughts. Much though I want to disregard his comments, I can't because he's right—we're not fit for this fight, and my magic isn't enough to pick up the slack. Our enemies wield supernatural powers that exceed my limited resources and skills.

But even though the prognosis looks bad, I still have a card or two up my sleeve. It won't be pretty and will cost me plenty, but there's no other solution now, even with Bowie busily restoring our troops to the fight.

Regardless, I must shelve all these problems and think about them later. Right now, Pene needs me more than anyone or anything does.

I carry the herbs back to camp.

Hannah, a young sprite who escaped Delerood with us, sits beside the supine Pene, pressing the thick wad of rags and spare clothes against the grievous wound. I expect the rags to be soaked with Pene's blood, but they manage to staunch the bleeding. I carefully clean the wound and then set to grinding my ingredients with a pestle as I imbue them with my own healing magic. Once I'm finished, I pack Pene's bandages with the poultice, and I don't fail to notice how fast Pene is fading.

"Hang in there," I urge her, stubbornly refusing

to accept the severity of her condition. "We're going to get you all fixed up."

"Don't waste your time on me, Belle," Pene whispers, shaking her head. "I can already hear the gods calling me home."

"Ignore them!" I protest, drawing all eyes to me. "We aren't ready to let you go. You still have… too much to keep you here."

With a strength that surprises me, she grabs my hand and squeezes it. Rather than speaking, she lets the truth shine through her eyes. Then she asks, "How about some of that strong ale the men keep in their flasks?"

Struggling to keep the tears from my eyes, I squeeze her hand in support. Brennan looks over my shoulder, watching our dying friend. I glance at him, clear my throat, and ask, "Can you fetch the strongest draught?"

He trots off without replying, approaching the men who are resting nearby. Many of them tend to their own lesser wounds. I look back at Pene after Brennan leaves, biting my lower lip and temporarily ignoring my sadness. It does no good for anyone to see me cry, least of all the person now dying before me.

"I'm so sorry, Pene," I whisper. "I wish I could have done more."

"Don't you dare mourn me, Belle," she spits back. "But I do want you to promise me something."

7

I swallow down my tears. "Anything."

"Redeem my pound of flesh. Don't let Morningstar win."

"I promise I'll do everything I can."

"I know you will," she says, her words punctuated by a sharp intake of breath. "You… you always do."

When Brennan returns with a flask of ale, he kneels down beside her and helps her raise her head to drink. As soon as he touches her, she releases a doleful howl of pain and he drops the flask so fast, he barely picks it up before all the contents spill on the ground. Pene's face reveals her extreme pain before her body finally relaxes, and all her torment vanishes. Her eyes fall on mine, and she fixes her blank stare on me as her soul is finally freed from the mortal confines of her body. I reach out to close her beautiful eyes, still stifling my tears, and Brennan rises to his feet.

My mind is full of pain and anger. Morningstar will pay for this!

Brennan breaks into my thoughts and asks, "What should we do with her?"

"We'll bury her here," I reply, my voice thick with emotion. "It's as close to home as we can get."

"Does she have any family we should notify?" he asks, looking down at her body. There's a soft smile lighting the ends of her lips and the pain that embraced her face earlier is nowhere to be seen.

She looks so peaceful in death.

"Her only family are the other orphans of war that banded together for this fight, and every one of them expects this kind of grave in the end."

"Well, I won't be surprised when more of us are buried here before this fight is all said and done," he answers.

"Your breach of faith benefits no one, Brennan," I scold him. The last thing I need right now is an uncommitted soldier. Although he's a brave warrior, Brennan can be also be a real bastard at times and we can't afford his way of thinking right now. "Tell the others we'll camp here tonight, and head out at first light," I command him. "Get a detail to give Pene a proper burial after you assign enough guards for the night watch."

He grimaces and walks away. As I see him return to camp, my thoughts start to run away with me. Nothing can change what happened. We can only make sure we're better prepared next time. If there is a next time…

The only way we can return to Delerood is if we bring someone with us who can bypass Kronos's time loop. Few can challenge that power, even fewer can surmount it, but I might stand a chance with the right backup. I nod to myself, reaffirming my decision.

###

When I return to camp, I find Brennan talking to a group of soldiers who bear less serious wounds. All of them are carrying shovels.

"For Pene?" I ask.

"Of course!" Brennan snaps, all the while glaring at me. "Any other orders?"

"Come morning, I will be leaving."

Understandably, he appears confused. "Why?"

"I need to go see some… old friends," I answer on a sigh.

"Doesn't sound like *friendly* old friends with the way you just said that."

That's because they're anything but friends. In fact, I'm more than sure they detest me. But what needs to be done, needs to be done. "That's beside the point."

"Then what is the point?"

I swallow hard. "They might know how we can get back into Delerood and then we can take the fight to Morningstar himself."

"We should go with you…" He inhales deeply. "*I* should go with you."

I shake my head. "This is something I must handle myself."

He doesn't appear at all convinced but sighs, acknowledging defeat. My stomach knots when he leaves. Despite everyone's frustration at how poorly we fared on the battlefield, it's good to know Brennan is still ready, able and willing to continue this fight. While I admire his stamina, I can't allow him or the others to accompany me on my quest. No, this is something between me and the three men whose lives I ruined.

I plan to rise very early in the morning, long before my comrades do, and then I'll leave before Brennan gets any ideas about following me.

First stop? I must go to the Hollows to replenish my supplies. After that, I'll head for Castle Chimera. This trip will be risky and I know I'll endure a great personal cost in return for their aid, but all judicious actions have their consequences.

And I'm long past due to atone for mine.

Chapter Two
Belle

At sundown, I arrive in the Hollows, where I take my respite at the inn.

I'm exhausted from the ride and grateful to sleep in a bed instead of on the ground. Even though I desperately need a good night's sleep, sleep doesn't come easily. Plaguing my mind are continuous nightmares that leave me tossing and turning all night. These are not mere bad dreams but a series of snippets chronicling the events that led to my cursing the prince and his two loyal followers.

And now I see the three of them, standing so proudly in battle. They come in, casting aside the wizards and witches that dare to stand up for themselves while the city is overtaken. As with all good lackeys of Morningstar, the three of them kill anything that tries to resist.

I spot them from afar, riding into battle on the backs of black stallions. They dismount and begin to cut a swath through the crowd, using their magic, dispatching the mob as if they were no more than clutter and debris to be swept away. They dominate the battle, stomping through the crowd as if they're invincible, demonstrating their prowess in battle by slaughtering the rebels by the bushel.

Sensing no remorse or regret, I watch in horror as they execute their dirty deeds in compliance with their dark leader, Kronos and their overlord, Morningstar. They are well aware the humans they butcher are inferior to them, which is vile beyond imagination.

Someone has to do something.

I gaze into the eyes of one wielding a sword. The prince. He wears a look of pure contempt as he trudges closer, but he doesn't faze me. One of the others notices me and follows his path. The air begins to tingle when one of them attempts to bludgeon me with magic, his power matching mine. He's shortly joined by another warrior. I fear getting locked into a time loop before I'm slain with his sword. Ironically, I have no time to lose if I'm to save the city. Summoning every ounce of power I can muster, I cast a spell on the three of them. They instantly disappear from sight, and I move on without a second thought.

I awaken with a start, and a sense of terrible unease haunts me. And why shouldn't it? In the sixteen years since that dreadful day, I've had dreams of the three men I cursed—three men who now roam the land as hideous creatures. For some reason, the nightmares are more vivid now than ever before. I can almost taste the putrid ash in the air from that awful day, a day I've since grown to regret because the truth of the matter is that I shouldn't have cursed them—or I shouldn't have allowed that curse to live on as long as it has.

I do believe people can change—that they can see the error in their ways and atone for those errors. And sixteen years locked to a castle and its surrounding grounds, cursed to roam as monsters is enough to cause someone to look back upon their mistakes and view them as such. It's the reason why I should have placed a time limit on my curse. But I was young and inexperienced then, and after the damage was done, I was stubbornly unable to face what I'd done. Now, I have no choice but to accept the consequences… sixteen years later.

Sometime before dawn, I finally abandon hope of sleep. Instead, I crawl out of bed and wash myself with water from a nearby bucket. After changing into fresh clothes, I head out to the local cemetery.

It's still dark outside when I silently traverse the streets before entering the ancient graveyard. The rusty gate creaks loudly and broadcasts my presence. I walk toward the far end of the cemetery before stopping in front of a row of graves. Sparing a moment to pick up the fallen branches and leaves that clutter the site, I sit down in the soft grass.

"Hello, Father; hello, Sister," I say to the headstones. I am no foreigner to the Hollows. Once, a long time ago, I called it home. "I know it's… been a while since I visited and for that, I am sorry." I pause and then take a deep breath as I shake my head and try to keep the tears at bay. "I just… I don't know if I'm doing the right thing," I tell them, all the while wondering what I'm even doing here. Even with my magic, I have no communication with the dead. "This war continues to drag on, and it seems as though it will never end." As I listen to the mournful notes of a nearby owl, I breathe deeply again. "I've already sacrificed so much, and failed so often, and I don't know why I'm still making mistakes. I don't even know if I'll survive the next battle, much less, if I even want to." I sigh as I look at either tombstone. "How I wish you were here so I could ask your advice."

I used to pity myself in the past because I had to mask my insecurity. I couldn't allow anyone to know any of the things I'd done—things I had to conceal. Admitting any flaws was a signal to those who followed me that I could be unfit—that I wasn't really the one worth following. And as a Chosen one, I couldn't allow that to happen. I had to keep up the guise—make everyone believe I had it all figured out, that I knew what I was doing.

As the Chosen few, we were picked to lead our people to victory, to overcome the evil that is Morningstar. And, yet, all the while, my people are being indiscriminately enslaved, tormented, cursed, incarcerated and routinely murdered. Of course they're frightened, but I'm just as petrified as they are, and I always have been. Though I can't admit it.

I was very young and inexperienced during the first war, barely twenty-years-old, and I had no idea how to control the immense power I possessed. It's taken me years to learn how to use it properly.

"I lost someone yesterday. Pene… she was so brave…"

The tears I never shed while watching Pene take her last breath finally surge forth and I'm helpless to restrain them. I sob quietly in the darkness, mourning another person on the long list of others I've failed to save and protect. Just like my family, lying here in front of me, it's too late now.

As my tears subside, I'm startled to realize I can no longer remember the features of my father or my sister, even as I fight to bring them to mind. I haven't forgotten them entirely, true, but I can no longer see their faces or recall the heart-warming sounds of their voices. They've, instead, been relegated to mere shadowy figures in the recesses of my mind. Will that also happen to my memory of Pene after enough time passes?

"No more!" I say, shaking my head. "I'm done with it. All of it! I'm done watching good people sacrifice their lives for a lost cause."

I stand up and try to suppress the rage that

suddenly ignites inside me. Instead, I think about the way in which I'll avenge them. What I have to do next will be painful, and maybe even fatal, but if I don't do it, even more will suffer. And I'm sick and tired of watching good people fighting for their own survival and… failing.

I sit in the darkness for a while as I think about all the decisions I've made up until this point, and I wonder at the decisions I'll still need to make. I know I made the right decision by sending the others back to their homes. I just don't want to see any more death—not anytime soon, anyway. I know death is coming—it's inevitable in the final battle against Morningstar. Perhaps the day will come, (if I survive), when all those who have gone will join me again, courtesy of Bowie's magic, and we will fight shoulder to shoulder once again, in the final battle.

I lay the roses I plucked from the garden outside the inn on each of the graves before me and then rise to my feet. The dawn turns the night sky gray. No more time for tears and uncertainty. My fate awaits me at Castle Chimera, and that fate lies in the hands of three men I hardly know yet three men to whom I did the ultimate disservice. Time to meet them face to face.

I return to the inn and pack my things hurriedly. Creeping back outside, I retrieve my horse from the stable and climb into the saddle. As the moon begins to fade and disappear, I point the mare in the direction of Castle Chimera. And I ride.

The sun is slow to rise, so the cover of darkness conceals me. All the while, my mind is a frantic mess. I miss my family and I want nothing more than to reunite with them once again. But I know that can never be.

My thoughts race as fast as my horse's hooves across the tundra. I don't know what will happen when I reach the castle—when I come face to face with the men I cursed… I can't imagine what their reactions will be. Now that I need them, it's imperative for me to make amends. To receive such forgiveness, I'm prepared to do whatever they ask.

Of course, I have to consider the chance they'll refuse me outright. Vengeance can run deep and in this case, I imagine it will. After all, living with my curse for nearly two decades might make them less than eager to return to the world outside the walls in which I confined them. Only one way to know for sure. No doubt, my powers of persuasion will be put to the test.

I can only hope they've repented their mistakes and no longer serve the interests of Kronos, Vita, and Morningstar. As they've been living in exile all this time and Morningstar made no motion to free them from my curse, I can't imagine they still place their allegiance with him, but one can never be too certain of anything.

Chapter Three
Alder

"I bet you wish you'd kept your ugly ass out of the castle, don't you?" I hiss at the malformed creature in front of me, which I've trapped in a corner of the basement. The beast looks at me with a mixture of fear and hate before I strike it again with my mace. A loud, cracking sound echoes through the cavernous path between the different chambers of the servants' quarters. Or what was once the servants' quarters—now they are long gone.

Looking at my mace, now cracked and splintered, I throw it away in disgust. Then I snarl at my *guest*, and the latest object of my fury, "What are you made of, iron?"

Unfortunately, I wasn't clever enough to figure out how the bloody thing managed to sneak into the castle in the first place. But torturing it proved absolutely useless. The only response I got for all my trouble were a few grunts and groans.

Frankly speaking, I'm not any easier on the eyes than the beast at my feet. But I wasn't always this way. After losing my fortune, I was summarily forced into Kronos's employ as a foot soldier. But at least then I still had my good looks. Women often fell at my feet. And having a good romp with a buxom maiden—or hell, *any* maiden—was never an obstacle or something I had trouble achieving. Now, not even the basest she-monster will lie with me!

Yes, I have become a truly pitiable sight. And not a day goes by that I don't threaten to kill the bitch that cursed me to this awful existence, that is, if I ever cross her path again. She'd better pray to whatever god she thinks will protect her that we never meet again. Arguably, sixteen years is a long time to nurture a grudge, but I've been managing it just fine.

The aberration jars me from my thoughts by grunting at me hoarsely again—when the bitch cursed me to this hideous monstrous form, she also cursed whatever creatures roamed within the castle. Who knows what this beast used to be? Fox? Rabbit? Rat?

Regardless, I'm at a loss as to what to do with it now? I could have just threatened it and driven it out, but I like to express my undying rage by keeping it in check. I strike the beast with the larger half of the broken mace, aiming the torn end at the monster yet again. This time, the weapon bounces back so fast, the sharp splinters nearly take off one of my three heads instead. The mace flies out of my grasp and lands on the floor with a deafening *clunk!*

I then find myself clenching my fists and debating whether a good punch will bring better results when a voice calls me from the stairs.

"For gods' sakes, Alder," Horatius sighs with exasperation. "Would you *stop* beating that pathetic thing and throw it out?"

I swivel my snake head to ask him, "And what sort of message would that send?"

"The same one you've been repeating for the last hour," Horatius replies, unimpressed. "*Stay out.* Besides, we both know the bloody thing's just hungry and looking for food."

This time, I turn my lion head around to face him, although I keep the eyes of my goat's head on the beast. "How about minding your own business?"

"It's difficult to mind my own business with the infernal racket you're making."

"Well, after the pounding I gave it, I'm sure it'll think twice before it crawls around scrounging again."

Horatius sighs with the weariness of a parent whose child won't learn. "Be that as it may, I thought I should mention something more important."

"And what is that?"

"Someone is approaching the castle."

That captures my attention, just as he knew it would. "Who?"

"I don't know yet. Appears to be a woman, but I can't say for sure."

"What makes you think it's a woman?"

"Educated guess," he grumbles. "Does it matter whether it's maid or man? Don't try to deny how much you love uninvited guests."

It irritates me to hear how well he knows me, but what should I expect after sharing a castle with him for sixteen years? I abandon the pitiful creature to make my way upstairs. Horatius walks past me, approaching the victim of my beating. I can hear him opening the trap door that lies halfway between the steps and the location where the creature is cornered.

"If you knew what was good for you, you would leave before he devises a way to finish you off," he tells the creature as though it understands a word coming from his mouth.

Regardless whether the wretch understands Horatius or not, the footsteps followed by a *clunk!* indicate the beast simply drops down the passage hole as instructed. I hear the trap door closing behind the thing before Horatius joins me at the top of the steps.

Soon, we're both looking out across the open field ahead of us. I can't see anything but the fog as it rolls in over the moors.

"You shouldn't have fed that damn thing in the first place," I grumble while I keep scanning the surroundings, still seeing nothing. "It'll just come back when it thinks the coast is clear, probably with more of its kind, whatever the hell it is."

Horatius shrugs, clearly indifferent and slightly annoyed. I want to punch him, simply on principle. "If such an unfortunate event happens, we'll deal with it. But I doubt it will."

"Oh?" I ask, frowning.

He nods. "You're one ugly son of a bitch that few can ever stomach seeing more than once."

"Last time I checked," I say, swiveling all my heads to face him. "You're not exactly on the A list, yourself."

"All the more reason for our uninvited guest to stay away, yes?"

Loath to lose yet another argument, I ask, "Where is this visitor you *thought* you saw?"

"Still coming," Horatius says. "But you're looking in the wrong place," he continues with a sly smile. "I saw a rider on *the other side* of the castle."

I glower at him. "You could have said that!"

"I could have," he replies with another dismissive shrug.

I channel all my anger and patiently turn around, preparing to walk the battlements to the flip side of the castle. Going down the stairs, I cross the castle center before charging out the front doors. I feel ready to greet the new arrival in my own terrifying way. Hopefully, my sudden, angry emergence through the doors will be quite enough to scare them off.

We don't do well with strangers.

The traveler's horse stops as soon as I emerge. My eyes glow as I focus on the beast. Horses are always such easy targets—they're so easily panicked. I charge toward it with a threatening snarl, upsetting the beast enough that it rears and loses its rider before recoiling in terror.

And that's when I take notice of the rider. A quick glance at her attire and petite figure confirms Horatius's assumption that she's female. I can't help but grin. Females, like horses, are always easy to terrify.

Though the castle is quite isolated, we do keep a stable of horses though I don't know why—it's not as though we ride them. But Horatius says he enjoys the beasts' company and he spends most of his time with them. The beasts won't come anywhere near me.

Much to my surprise, the woman seems unfazed by my theatrics. She rises from the ground and rearranges her long cloak as if she merely tripped. I immediately notice something familiar about her. And that familiarity makes the bile rise in my throat, though I still can't place her.

After turning to face me, she pulls back her hood and I realize why she seems so familiar. It's the bitch who cursed me!

Everything around me suddenly begins to bleed red as anger blanches through me. A second later, I launch myself at her. Never mind trying to scare her. I intend to rip her apart limb from limb before sticking her head on a spike as a warning to others of her ilk. I'm almost upon her when I crash into an invisible brick wall, judging by the feel of it. I'm suspended in mid-air, my body floating weightlessly.

I want to yell my outrage at her, but she can't understand a word of it. To anyone except Horatius and Beacon, my words come out as grunts and groans, similar to those of the beast I just drove out. Of all the pain and inconveniences I've undergone since becoming cursed to this miserable place, losing my speech was the least of my regrets, until now. Oh, how I'd give anything for a voice just so I could explain in detail all the rotten things unfit for a woman's ears that I would do to her. Despite her good looks and curvy figure, she's hardly a woman in my eyes. She's the foulest of all witches.

Out of the corner of my eye, I see Horatius. When he gives me a curious look, I tell him, "The bitch froze me! I don't know how she did it!" No sooner do I say the words when I hear and see Beacon standing on my right. I'm barely able to think straight. The more I try to move, the less I can and the angrier I become.

"Good," the woman says in a casual tone. "Now that you're all here, I'd like to have a little chat with you… inside." She gives us a knowing look. "As long as all of you promise to behave?"

"And why would we agree to that?" Horatius asks, and it appears the witch understands him.

"Because I'm about to offer you redemption," she says.

"Fuck off," I start, but Horatius shakes his head at me.

"We're interested in listening," Beacon says as she faces him and gives a curt nod.

The ensuing minutes grow long and tense before both of them nod in return at her. In an instant, she ends the spell, dropping me on the ground and I fall as though I'm an anchor. I start to rise and fully intend to rush her again, but she holds up one hand to freeze me in place again.

"I wouldn't, Prince Alder," she says with a heavier note of warning. "I can make you far more hideous than you are right now and cripple you, besides. Is that what you want?"

How long has it been since anyone addressed me by my proper title? The words sound so sweet to my ragged ears. Even coming from her mouth, they strike a chord in me and I respond by grunting my agreement.

"Good," she says, lowering her hand. "I knew the man was still inside the beast somewhere." She looks at Horatius and Beacon. "With you two, there were never any doubts." She looks at me again and sighs. "Now, shall we go inside? I have a proposition to make to all three of you."

When we affirm with our signature grunts, she asks us to follow her inside.

Oh, yes, I'll listen to her proposition, just out of idle curiosity.

And once my curiosity's fully satisfied, I'll kill her!

Chapter Four
Belle

After I release Alder from the suspended animation spell, I still maintain my compulsion on him and the others.

Maybe it's not the best way to open a conversation, but it prevents them from tearing me apart before they've heard everything I have to say. I sense their collective anger rolling off them in waves. After so many years of enduring all the repercussions of my curse, I can hardly fault them. I can only hope my offer falls on open ears—yes, I could compel them to agree with me and do my bidding, but that compulsion would only last so long and then they'd realized they'd been duped and probably be even angrier with me than they already are. No, the only way forward is for them to agree to my terms of their own free will.

The longer I look at them, the guiltier I feel. Like my family, the features and details of their faces have faded into the dusty corridors of my memory. The only thing I do remember about these three men, prior to my curse, was how large, handsome and virile they were when they were men. Now they're three of the most hideous creatures my imagination at the time could conjure up—Alder is a chimera, Horatius is an ogre and Beacon is a cyclops. How horrible must it be to have lived and continue to live like such pariahs? Well, I'm about to offer them the chance to start anew.

We stop in the courtyard, and I ask them all to face me. While I hold my compelling spell with one hand, I use the other to weave a rune in the air.

Horatius looks at me in alarm.

"This is just a language spell I'm weaving," I explain. "It will allow you to communicate with me in something more intelligible than grunts." Yes, I could somewhat understand them before, using my *Beast Sense* abilities, but this will make communication significantly easier.

I finish the motion and the glyph glows in the air. Beacon grunts, and I'm fearful the spell didn't work.

Then he says, "Why are you here, witch?"

"To deactivate the curse I put on each of you," I respond. As expected, all of them look at each other in various expressions of disbelief and anger. Alder is the angriest, but that's to be expected.

Beacon speaks first and asks, "Why, after all this time, would you offer to break this curse now?"

"I have my reasons," I reply and then swallow hard.

"What are those reasons?" Alder demands.

I turn to look at him. "Reasons I'm unable to share with you presently."

Alder snarls through his three sets of gnashing teeth. "This is nothing more than a trick. You've simply come to ensure we are as miserable as you left us."

"Why would I waste my time on such an errand?" I shrug, taking the time to fiercely match all three glares he casts at me. "What could I possibly gain in coming here to trick you?"

"With all due respect," Horatius says slowly, "I doubt you're here strictly in the name of charity."

"Yes and no," I respond.

"Explain," Alder says.

I nod. "Before I leave, I promise to disengage the curse I placed on all of you, regardless of your cooperation or not." I raise a finger. "However, unless you accept my terms, there is one part of the curse that will remain in effect."

"And which part is that?"

"You will continue to be unable to leave the boundaries of the surrounding woods."

Alder snips, "Always the little things that make our misery so lasting."

After throwing Alder an irritated expression, Horatius asks, "And what are your terms?"

"Your old commander, Kronos and his henchwoman, Vita, are waging war once more," I explain. "And I intend to defeat them." I clear my throat. "In order to defeat them, I need your help."

"Our help?" Beacon repeats doubtfully as Alder shakes all three of his heads and all three of his mouths laugh in unison.

"Who better to help me than three of Kronos' most trusted warriors?" I ask, forcing my attention to remain on Beacon. If I can convince Horatius and Beacon to agree, I'll have more luck with Alder. "You might succeed where others failed."

"Why should we help you?" Horatius asks, frowning at me. "Assuming you're telling the truth about lifting the curse regardless of whether or not we assist you, we could just choose to live out the rest of our days here… as humans."

"Yes, you would be free of the monster part of the curse, but you wouldn't be *free*. Your true freedom would still be… mine."

"What's stopping us from simply threatening to tear you apart unless you fully remove both curses?" Alder demands.

"Because, in case you've forgotten, I still possess magic."

"Convenient," Alder grumbles.

"So, the only way we would earn our freedom is to fight against Kronos?" Beacon asks.

I look at him and nod. "Thus, the question now becomes one of loyalty. How devoted are you to Kronos?"

Alder laughs at that. "We were never loyal to him."

"Yet you sided with him." I spit the words back into his face.

"We have all made our own mistakes," Horatius answers as he fixes me with a penetrating gaze.

"Then your loyalties," I start.

"Don't lie with Kronos," Beacon finishes.

"He can rot in hell for all eternity for all we care," Alder adds. Clearly, their anger doesn't just extend to me.

"Then what's stopping you from agreeing to my offer?" I ask.

Alder takes a step closer to me. "Have you forgotten what you did to us? Do you have any idea how much hatred we have for you? Have you forgotten about the fact that you destroyed our lives?" he hisses, all three of his mouths speaking at the same time.

I take a deep breath. "At the time, you were my enemies."

"And we aren't now?" Alder laughs.

"I'm offering you peace," I say, narrowing my eyes.

"And what of my need for vengeance?" he demands, then motions to the other two. "*Our* need for vengeance?"

"I… I don't know what you want me to say. I'm offering you the chance for redemption—to make good on your mistakes of the past."

He chuckles. "I don't give a fuck about my

mistakes of the past."

I look at his lion head, the one that seems to be dominant. "Then what do you give a fuck about?"

"Vengeance," he hisses the word. "In order to earn my assistance for your cause, I require you to allow me to slake my vengeance on you."

I swallow hard. "What does that mean?"

"Whatever I want it to mean."

"Alder," Horatius starts. "She is offering us a chance to break this curse."

"I know what she's offering!" Alder yells. "And breaking this curse won't do a damn thing about the anger that's been burning inside me for sixteen fucking years!"

"Yes," I agree in a winded breath as I realize the lives of my soldiers rest on this decision here and now. I need Alder if I'm going to move forward with the rest of my plan. "Yes, I'll submit myself to your vengeance," I continue as I look at the others. "I know all of you have an axe to grind with me over your curse."

"Give me half a chance," one of Alder's heads snaps, "and I'll show you how sharp that axe is."

"Then that's exactly what I will do," I calmly reply.

Alder looks at me in confusion. "Explain."

"If you agree to help me, you can do whatever you want to me in order to avenge your hatred and anger for me."

Horatius appears surprised and I can't read

Beacon's expression. Alder appears delighted, but then that delight is replaced with suspicion.

"Anything?" Alder asks.

I nod. "Anything short of killing me."

He breathes in deeply and then nods all three of his heads.

"After you do whatever it is you want to me, however," I continue. "We agree to call a truce and get on with *my plan.*"

"In that case, I accept your deal," Alder says with a hideous trio of lurid smiles. "I've been dreaming about getting my hands on you for a *very* long time."

"Wait!" Horatius interrupts, looking at him with angry eyes. "Don't you think we should talk about this before you agree to it?"

"What's there to talk about?" Alder demands on a shrug. "We get our lives back and we also get to take out every ounce of rage we've ever harbored for that fucking bitch," he finishes and glares at me.

"And suppose we aren't interested in torture?" Beacon asks. Of the three of them, he always struck me as the least detestable. Perhaps he was tied with Horatius.

"Why wouldn't you be?" Alder retorts, shaking his heads as if he can't understand Beacon. "You want to live the rest of your life walking around with one bloodshot eye, a puckered orifice with broken, yellow, jagged teeth, looking forward to a steady diet of potatoes, rodents and whatever we can scrape together with our bare hands?"

"I say all that's preferable to giving the witch whatever she wants," Horatius protests, but we both know it's a lost cause. The previous anger I felt from all of them is dissipating, replaced with the faint glimmer of hope.

"Fine," Beacon sighs at Alder. "I agree to her terms."

Alder nods his three heads in satisfaction before looking up at Horatius.

"Alright," the latter says, throwing up his hands.

Horatius proffers his enormous ogre hand. I take it and we shake in agreement. I note the claw-like grip with which he squeezes my fingers. My hand is practically numb by the time he releases it. When I glance over at Beacon, he waves his hand at me and I say, "One handshake is enough for me."

I glance at Alder, who looks sickeningly predatory, and his eyes glow with unmasked eagerness. I might as well prepare myself for the worst beating of my life. To say nothing of the most degrading sexual experience that will surely accompany it. I take another deep breath before raising my hand in the air, then I say the ancient words while using my fingers to trace out yet another glyph.

Their transformation is immediate.

Within the blink of an eye, I'm suddenly looking at three faces I've not seen in a long time. Each man is naked, unusually handsome and to their benefit, all are well-endowed. When last I saw them, sixteen years ago, they were clothed in heavy armor, so I never saw how gorgeous they actually were. And now that I do, I find myself swallowing hard.

Alder is the tallest of them, Horatius and Beacon tied and all easily tower over me. Alder's hair is long and dark to match his dark eyes. With his chiseled features, strong nose and jaw and olive complexion, he looks as though he hails from the Anoka desert. Beacon, is quite the opposite with a sculptured face, fair hair and blue eyes. He has the look of someone elven. And Horatius is storybook handsome—light brown hair that curls over his ears and matches the shadow that covers his jaw. His eyes appear to be emeralds in his face.

How is it that I can more easily look upon their monster counterparts than I can their actual human forms?

"You are returned to your true selves, as I promised," I say with a quick nod. "I'll make good on the other part of my deal, freeing you from the confines of the castle grounds, when it's time for us to defeat Kronos and Morningstar."

Horatius's initial elation fades from his face. "You didn't say anything about going up against Morningstar."

"I'm saying it now," I point out. "And certainly you knew who Kronos' ultimate master is?"

"I didn't become human again just to commit suicide on the battlefield," Horatius protests.

"Morningstar is more powerful than any of us," Beacon concurs.

"Let me worry about Morningstar," I tell him. "I just want you to focus on Kronos, Vita, and the others within their ranks."

Horatius scoffs. "As if it were that easy! I know more about Kronos' power than anyone alive and I can safely say we're not even close to ready for any conflict with either of them."

I bubble with anger. "So, are you saying the deal is off, then? All because you're too scared of Kronos?"

"We're not scared of anyone!" Alder roars with righteous anger. I try to avoid staring at his manhood when it shakes violently with his rage. I try and I fail and immediately feel a blush steal across my cheeks.

"My eyes are up here, witch," Alder spits at me, his handsome face breaking into an evil smile.

"Maybe you aren't scared of anything," I reply, wishing the embarrassment would flee from my expression, "but Horatius seems to have a different opinion."

Alder glares at his companion. "You always were too timid for your own bloody good."

"And you are much too reckless for yours,"

Horatius counters.

"Doesn't he raise a good point, though?"
Beacon chimes in.

Alder grunts at both of his companions. "If you
wish to gain your freedom from this blasted place,
we have no choice in the matter."

Beacon and Horatius glance at each other
doubtfully. Then Horatius says to me, "You'll stay
true to your word? If we help you against Kronos
and we live, you'll allow us to remain human? And
you'll gift us our freedom from this castle?"

I raise my still-numb fingers. "By all I hold
holy, yes, that is so."

Alder's face splits into a wolfish smile. "Good
enough for me."

With one fluid motion, he lunges forward to
grab hold of my hair. It takes all the self-control I
have to let him pull my head back, and then his lips
are on mine and his tongue is in my mouth. He
kisses me violently before ripping his lips away.

"And now I will see to that vengeance you
promised me, witch," he spits the words at me and,
gripping me around the waist, hauls me up the
nearby staircase.

"Remember, there's no bargain if she's dead,"
Horatius calls out behind him, frowning. Alder
says nothing as he carries me up the steps.

While it's not clear what he fully plans to do to
me, his rough kiss gives me hope. I think he just
plans to have sex with me. Of course, the sex won't

be gentle, but he could just as easily have opted for the dungeons, where the torture devices are plentiful and varied. And painful.

Despite the circumstances, I feel slightly excited, though I'm stunned as to why. I'm no virgin, but I've had very few sexual partners. In fact, it's been at least five years since I've been with a man.

Just get through this, Belle, I tell myself. *And realize it was something that had to happen in order to convince Alder to do your bidding.*

But Alder isn't the only one who will take out his rage and, most probably, his lust on me. I must also allow Beacon and Horatius to do whatever they choose to me when it's their turn. Alder's intentions seem pretty clear, but I sense he's far more brutal than the other two.

Better to get Alder out of the way first.

He pushes the heavy oak door to a bed chamber open and throws me into the room. I trip over my own feet and land on the floor. The room we enter is in shambles, although the bed itself is pristine. I realize all at once why: what use is a comfortable bed to a chimera? The pile of blankets in one corner looks more like the typical nest for such a creature. My guess is confirmed when Alder grips me by the arm and drags me across the room, throwing me onto the pile. A twisted smile splits his lips as I look up and prepare myself for whatever he might do next.

Chapter Five
Belle

"Take your clothing off," Alder commands.

I obey—since it's my choice to be here. Because I must be, I can be submissive. I stand up and unbutton my trousers, pulling them down my legs. Then I untie my linen tunic and yank it over my head. Clad only in my camisole and panties, I can feel my nipples hardening under the impertinence of his stare and what's even odder is the sting between my legs that tells me I'm growing wet for him.

Of course, I don't understand why.

I meet his gaze while removing my camisole, and even though his eyes are filled with lust, I can sense he's not ready to mate me yet. No, he wants to humiliate me first, to degrade me.

"Don't look at me!" he growls at me. "Lower your head! Show me the damned respect I'm due! I'm a prince, or have you forgotten?"

I breathe in deeply. "I haven't forgotten."

I drop my eyes as he walks toward the wall behind me. Hanging on a peg is a thin horse whip, which he retrieves and then, walking back towards

me, uses it to gently caress the flesh of my
shoulders. He pulls the whip away before cracking
the air with it and, in response, I jump. The smell
of the well-used leather makes me flinch, despite
my continued effort to appear calm. The thought of
the harsh whip hitting my skin makes me ill. Yes, I
could shield myself with my own magic, but I
don't want to. I can't explain why, but I almost feel
as if this beating he's sure to give me is going to
allow me my own sense of reprieve from the guilt
I've been harboring over the three of them these
sixteen years.

"You're afraid of me," he says the words in a
victorious tone.

And that's when anger begins to bubble up
within me. He can do what he wants with me, but
I'm not going to allow him to think he's won. I'm
going to maintain my own inner strength,
regardless of what he does to my body.

"No."

Fearing him isn't an option because I can't
show him weakness. I have to stand up to my
punishment, and I have to take the beatings in my
stride. Even the mating. I give him a crooked smile
and pretend indifference. "So," I say as I observe
him. "Do you plan to flog me or mate me?"

A hearty chuckle bubbles up from his throat.
"Both in good time." Then his free hand seizes me
under the jaw and he snarls, "Now shut your
mouth."

I'm usually the one in control and I don't like feeling helpless. It's very odd to view oneself as an object, an instrument of pleasure to be used, and, more dangerously, abused. And, yet, there's something else inside me that thrills at the idea of him inside me.

He roughly pulls his hand off my jaw and commands me, "Take off your panties very slowly."

His order is quieter than before, almost a whisper. I don't sense the slightest hint of desire in his tone, only his expectation to be silently obeyed. My traitorous body is enticed by his terse order, and I can feel my sex growing wetter. I keep my head down, and hook my fingers into either side of my lace underclothes, dragging out the effort as long as possible. When I let the panties slip to the floor, I carefully extricate my feet, delaying the inevitable.

"Stop," he says, raising the whip to my face.

I freeze in place as he places the whip on the back of my neck and presses it into my skin as he says, "Kneel."

Dropping down to my knees, I can only wonder what will happen next. My answer comes fast enough. The whip cracks, striking my naked breasts, and leaving a long red stripe across them. I cry out at the unexpected assault and the pain.

"That's for cursing me to the most wretched of existences."

The lash burns my tender skin, and tears threaten my eyes. He cracks the whip again, but this time not quite so hard. The end of the whip catches me right between my legs, snaring the side of my inner thigh. I bite my lip to keep from crying out again.

"Up," he snarls, pushing the whip under my chin. My jaw clenches tightly as I do what he says, my heart pounding in my chest.

"Turn around."

I steel myself for the blows I know will come. My back is turned to him, but I can still see him in my mind's eye, and I know he's leering over my naked form. Anticipation and fear for his next blow nearly overtakes me, and I raise my head slightly to prepare myself for the forthcoming assault.

The whip cracks right next to my left ear, but he doesn't strike me.

"Keep your head down!" he bellows. "You will submit to me and allow me to do whatever I want to you, whenever I want it. Understand?"

"Yes," I whisper.

He suddenly grabs my arms and, picking up a stray piece of rope from the floor, quickly binds my hands behind me. Pulling a nearby chair over to sit on, he throws me over his lap and raises his hand, bringing it firmly down on my backside as I scream out in pain. He ruthlessly spanks me repeatedly. The blows become increasingly harder, no doubt, branding a large, angry handprint on my bottom.

"What you did to us was wrong," he says.

"I know," I answer. "And I'm sorry for it."

"I don't want to hear your fucking apologies," he growls. "I don't believe them."

"You might not believe them, but they're true."

He smacks me as hard as he can across my bottom, and I bite down on my lower lip to keep from crying out.

"And yet you only returned when you required our assistance," he chuckles as he then begins rubbing my cheeks as though trying to heal the sting of his assault.

"I thought about returning many times," I say, my voice coming out breathy.

He stops rubbing me and smacks me again as I yelp my shock. Then, before I can be fully aware of what he's doing, I feel his fingers pushing apart my folds, his index finger pushing just the tip inside me. He chuckles.

"You're wet," he says and I feel myself swallow hard. "You're enjoying this beating, aren't you?"

"No... no," I manage.

"And yet your pussy says otherwise." He pushes his finger all the way inside me and I can't help the moan that escapes my mouth. He spanks me again. "I don't want you to enjoy this."

He pulls his finger out and slams his palm against my ass again. I bite my lip to keep from crying out. It's not because of the pain. I've suffered countless battle wounds that were infinitely worse than this. No, the cry is simply an urgent need to release my humiliation and shame. When I finally dare to let out a small whimper, Alder cuts it off by stuffing a filthy handkerchief into my mouth before yanking my head sharply backward.

"I told you to keep your mouth shut," he snarls angrily. "You must require a few more blows to really grind the lesson in." He then folds me across his lap again and continues his cruel assault on my backside, alternating with shoving his finger inside me as if to judge whether his attack is still turning me on.

"Mmm, you still like it. You want my cock, don't you, witch?"

For a moment, I feel beyond angry, and I'm even prepared to renege on the whole deal and take my chances with Morningstar. Getting beaten and mounted are one thing, but he's playing with me, humiliating me to enhance his own sickening pleasure. It's almost enough to make me seriously consider turning him back into the beast he was. But, no, I need him. I need all three of them.

He throws me off his lap, my bound hands ensuring I land ungraciously on the floor. The pain only further aggravates my sore bottom.

"Stand up," he demands with an impatient wave of his hand.

46

I struggle to get to my feet, but I eventually manage. No sooner have I risen, then he slaps my tender backside again. I shiver from the blow and mentally renew my vows of hatred for him.

"Walk in front of me," he orders. "Walk to the far wall and then back again."

He watches me, alternating his gaze between my breasts and my sex, which, even now, is dripping for his touch. And I'm beyond humiliated that such is the case.

For the next hour or so, I do exactly as he commands while he watches me with a blend of anger and victory in his eyes. I'm careful to obey each order with perfect discipline.

He remains terse and direct: "Stop. Sit down. Rise. Spread your legs. Touch yourself." Every demand is accompanied by slaps and blows to my breasts, stomach, back, legs and ass. Sometimes he uses his hand, and other times, the whip. After a while, the pain becomes easier to bear. The humiliation is much more intense.

Finally, he orders me to get on my hands and knees. I expect him to shove his cock down my throat and make me service him with my mouth. Much to my surprise, however, he drags me up onto the bed. Shoving my legs apart, he ties my ankles to the bedposts before pulling me backward and raising my ass up in the air.

I brace myself for another spanking, only this time, with the whip. But instead of feeling the sting of the leather, I feel the head of the handle of the whip as he rubs it across my swollen sex. He centers the rounded wood against my sensitive nub, and I can't help but moan out as my hips begin to gyrate of their own accord.

"Mmm, I never thought the witch was also a whore," he chuckles.

I can't bring myself to care and I hate it. I hate the fact that my body wants nothing more than to feel his throbbing cock inside it. I want him to mate me—what's more, I *need* it.

"You want me to fuck you, don't you?" he demands as he rips the binding from my mouth.

I can't bring myself to answer.

"Respond!"

"Y… yes," I answer on a whimper as he pushes the handle of the whip into me just a fraction. At his chuckle, I feel myself flush with indignation.

"Then I suppose I should oblige."

He drapes the offending weapon across my back, and a second later, I feel his engorged cock slamming into me in one thrust. I can't help but yelp as I lurch forward, but he holds me in place as he proceeds to mount me as hard as he can. I'm unprepared for it at first, and I tense and tremble. I can feel him stretching my insides with the brute force of his rapid, successive thrusts. I clamp my jaw and press my face hard into the mattress because I don't want him to hear the moans of pleasure I'm doing my best to suppress.

I want this!

I don't understand why or how, but the fact remains. I love the feel of his cock as he pushes inside me as hard as he can. He's trying to hurt me, I know that, and his strokes are hard and fast, but my body only wants more. The sensations of raw pleasure heighten as my disloyal body betrays me. I respond to his cruelty and writhe on the bed, unable to disengage myself from the hate he inflicts on me. When an orgasm more powerful than anything I've ever felt racks my body, I explode into a thousand flaming suns.

"You like being fucked like a common trollop, don't you?" he gloats behind me before increasing the speed and impact of his incessant strokes. He seems to delight in slamming himself violently inside me. I hear him moan loudly as he buries himself in me one last time, and I can feel his seed filling me. As he pulls free, I don't dare move.

He unties my ankles and my wrists.

"Are we done?" I ask, my voice sounding as raw as sandpaper.

His nasty smile comes back with a vengeance. "No, we're not done! Not by a long shot." Then he starts to chuckle as he turns my chin up so I'm forced to look at him. "You're going to clean up my cock with your tongue and get me good and hard again."

"After all that?" I stupidly ask in amazement.

His hand grips my jaw, and he replies, "For sixteen years, I've been celibate, shunned by any and all women. I have some catching up to do and you'll serve my purposes well." The grin returns. "Good thing you're so easy to look at."

I start to feel afraid. "I never agreed to letting you have me all night."

"There was no time limit set in your bargain," he answers on an acidic laugh. "Our contract allows me to do whatever I want to you, whenever I want to." He gets close enough for me to feel his breath against my cheeks. "What I want right now is to fuck you until I can't get it up again." Putting his hand around my throat, he yanks me toward him and then drops his mouth on mine in a rough kiss that bruises my lips. When he releases me, he says, "Keep doing what you're told."

After that, time ceases to exist. I quickly lose count of how many ways he mates me and how many times I orgasm, before he finally passes out. Daylight is still hours away. I'm sore in so many places and I can barely walk. Carefully climbing out of the bed, I gingerly wash myself using the water basin. After I put my clothes back on, I silently leave the room.

In the corridor, I take a deep breath and reflect on my ordeal. I've walked away from many battles feeling much less sore and yet, I can't say I didn't enjoy what just passed between us—even the beatings, strangely. Everything hurts and my nightmare is far from over and yet, there's something within me that wants more—that wants to understand what retribution will look like from Horatius and Beacon.

What in the bloody hell is wrong with me? I don't have an answer for myself.

Chapter Six
Belle

Despite not looking forward to whatever he has planned for me, I seek out Beacon the next morning.

I can hardly walk after last night with Prince Alder, but I must keep my word—to all three of them. I'm beyond relieved to be done with Alder and my payment to him, though I must admit, the memories of him inside me haven't left my mind. Even though the sex was rough, I can't deny the fact that I enjoyed it. And I'm not sure what that says about me because it was clear Alder was using me for his own enjoyment. And there were moments—more than one—that he attempted to humiliate me and succeeded. Sharing my body with him was nothing like sex has been in the past—with other men. There was none of the kindness, or the romance I'm accustomed to. Sex with Alder was violent, feral and animalistic and yet, I can't recall another sexual incident that refused to leave my mind.

Shaking the memories away, I find Beacon standing in his room, with the door slightly ajar.

From what I can tell, he's gazing at a painting on the wall. He's dressed, but the style of his clothing is quite outdated, owing to the fact that he's not been able to update his closet in sixteen years.

Regardless, he's still incredibly handsome with his white-blond hair that cascades to his shoulders, drawing my eyes to the thin fabric of his moth-eaten shirt. It seems the only creatures that have had access to his clothing are of the insect variety. Even so, he still cuts a dashing figure. Curiously, his feet remain bare.

I also notice that he's opened every dirt-caked window in the dark, dingy room, allowing the daylight in. I clear my throat to let him know I'm standing here, right outside his door, but he makes no move to acknowledge my presence. Instead, he turns from the painting on the wall and fixes his stare on the landscape outside his window, ignoring me.

"I have given Alder the retribution he desired from me," I say loud enough for the words to echo across the stone walls of the room as I enter and close the door behind me. If what Beacon wants from me is of a physical nature, I'd like to have our privacy. "What do you want from me in the name of your own retribution?"

"Nothing," he says, turning to face me with a shrug as I frown, not sure I'm following.

"Nothing?"

He nods. "Unlike Alder, there's nothing you

can give me that would remove the damage within me by your curse."

I breathe in deeply. "Certainly you are angry with me?"

He chuckles and nods. "What Alder will quickly come to realize is that anger doesn't vanish with ejaculation."

I swallow hard as the word brings to mind how many times Alder did just that. "Then," I start, but he interrupts.

"I wouldn't sully myself sexually with you. The things I want are nothing you could ever give me."

I'm taken aback by his stern refusal. I'm also mesmerized by the color of his pale blue eyes, which shimmer and appear almost white in the bright light of day. They're quite breathtaking, as is he. He appears younger than Alder and Horatius, but he's also less stocky than the other two—his is a long and lanky sort of muscle.

"Ask me," I challenge him, eager to get this payback business finally finished. I want a clean slate because otherwise, I know they won't agree to accompanying me to the final battle with Morningstar. "What do you want?"

In an instant, he walks over to stand right in front of me and his previously placid light eyes are now brewing with anger. "The only thing I want is my sister," he barks, eyes narrowing as his jaw locks. "And I doubt you can help remedy that situation."

"Where is she?" I ask, keeping my tone calm in an effort to temper his obvious anger. I must placate the three of them, not fight them. The time for angry words is over and now it's about making amends for the past, so I can ensure Fantasia has a future.

"I don't know," he admits, cooling a little as he inhales deeply while shaking his head. "I've been stuck in this castle for sixteen years, always awaiting the day someone might break the spell so I could venture out and find my kin." His blue eyes spark a little as he adds, "Yet, now that you're here and I'm human again, I can't even do that."

"I still promised you your own vengeance against me as a way to heal your anger."

"Don't confuse me with Alder," he spits the words at me. "I'm angry at you, of course. But what good is punishing you? Doing so can't bring my sister back or the sixteen years I've lost. How could beating you possibly make me feel any better?" He chuckles then as he shakes his head. "And mating you? No… you're not my type of woman."

I swallow hard and try not to feel offended, but I can't seem to help it, which is an odd reaction because I shouldn't give a damn what sort of woman he's attracted to and yet… yet I do. "And what kind of woman is that?"

"A woman with heart." He looks down at my

chest then and shakes his head. "After what you've done to us, what you put us through, you obviously have none."

I bite my lip to avoid saying the harsh words I'm thinking—that I simply did what I had to do at the time—that he seems to have conveniently forgotten that he was my enemy, fighting for Morningstar. And that because of Morningstar and his soldiers, soldiers just like Beacon, my family is dead.

But I need him. I need all three of them and defensive, angry conversations aren't going to get me any closer to my goal.

Not to mention, I don't fully believe him. Despite what he says, all men want something. If his sister is still alive, perhaps I can help him find her when this battle is all said and done (as long as we're still alive, that is).

He looks at me as if seeing me for the first time. He doesn't look as though he likes what he sees. "So, I will repeat—no, there is nothing you can do for me. You destroyed my life—that was quite enough."

"Must I remind you that sixteen years ago you were an agent of Kronos," I start but he interrupts me as he takes a step nearer and shakes his head, his eyes suddenly fuming.

"Sixteen years is a long time!" he yells back at me. "And in those sixteen years that I've been imprisoned here, I've learned to regret my actions."

He breathes in deeply as he turns away from me and shakes his head, his voice much lower as he continues, "It was a situation I never wanted to be in in the first place, but once I found myself in his ranks, I had to obey him, because if I didn't, he would kill me. I promised myself I would remain alive simply so I could find my sister again." He takes a breath. "I was forced to do things I did in Kronos' name because there was no other option."

"That was of no fault of anyone but," I start, but he holds up a hand, which is just as well because I'm not doing a very good job of remaining cool and collected.

"It was no one's fault, but my own. And I've had plenty of time to regret that decision and the countless decisions that came after. Yet, you left the three of us here to rot, regardless of how much we'd atoned for our sins of the past."

"I'm here now."

He nods. "Because you want something from us."

I can't argue with that, so I don't try. Instead, I breathe out a frustrated sigh. "Tell me about your sister. Perhaps I might still be able to help."

"I lost touch with her when Kronos forced me into his army. Later, I tried to go back to find her, but by then she was long gone. Then you came along, taking away the only chance I had of reaching my sister." He swallows visibly before saying, "The odds are pretty high that she's dead.

But I still want to know what exactly became of her in the hopes that… well, that she's still alive and well."

I have to agree with his assessment. If his sister has been on her own all this time, there's little chance she might have survived. As long as Beacon can't confirm her death, however, his small glimmer of hope remains, and it's a glimmer I want to kindle, because it appears to be the only way I can get him to help me.

While I try to work out some kind of compromise with him in my head, he says, "Thanks to you and your curse, I failed in my effort to save my sister."

"That's hardly," I start, but he interrupts.

"I blame her death on you."

"Don't be so quick to cast stones," I snap, my sudden surge of anger probably destroying any chance that he might have helped me. "My father died of a heart attack when your army invaded our land," I continue, wanting and needing him to understand that his isn't the only sad tale of woe and misery. "My sister was trampled to death by their heavy boots when your comrades arrived to slaughter us all. So, while you *might* have lost your sister, I *did* lose my father and my sister—the only family I had left." I take a deep breath and I can feel the sting of my own words, as well as the anger. "As far as I'm concerned, you, Alder, and Horatius could have cut my father and sister down with your swords." I take a breath. "The point is, we all have our own stories of suffering and woe. You aren't the only one."

I turn to leave, feeling angrier than I thought possible. The fact that I might have just blown my chance to get Beacon's assistance barely crosses my mind. I just, I can't stand the fact that all three of them act as though only their pain matters. It doesn't!

Beacon stops me by grabbing my arm, and then he twirls me back around to face him. He says nothing for a few seconds but then backs me against the nearest wall and I suddenly wonder if he's going to hit me—the coronas of his eyes burn with pain that surprises me.

"I don't doubt what you said," he tells me, his voice low and controlled, deep. "But how dare you think you can just suddenly appear here with promises to remove the curse!"

"Promises? I removed it."

He nods. "As if our becoming human again is enough to make everything return to the way it was before! You act as though this one act should be enough to wash away years of solitude, of loneliness, of loss." As he speaks, his tone rises, and the anger seeps through his words. "Your audacity is alarming. Don't you realize it's too late to simply make everything better?"

"Are you or are you not human again?"

He further narrows his eyes. "We may be

humans again, but our lives are hopelessly ruined."

"And what about all the innocent people whose lives *you* ruined?" I argue, glaring at him. "How many more lives would have been lost if I hadn't cursed and exiled the three of you when I did?" I feel my own fire starting to kick up again and I push away from him, but he reaches out and grabs my arm. "You feel sorry for yourself and your sister, but what about the other families you destroyed? What about *my* family?"

Once more, his anger cools. "I had no choice in the matter. I had orders, and those orders were to fight the enemy."

"I had orders, as well."

"You turned us into monsters," he says, his voice still quiet but filled with accusation.

"You deserved it."

He flinches as though I've slapped him. When he releases my arm, I jerk away, turning and running out of the room before I say or do something else I'll regret. Everything I see is angry red and I know better than to try to calm myself down at this point. Only time will allow that to happen.

I don't stop running away until I'm outside the castle walls and standing in the courtyard, breathing the fresh air deeply in an attempt to clear my head.

This errand is turning out to be much more difficult than I estimated. Naturally, I anticipated their hateful dispositions, however, I failed to realize how mutual that feeling is. I wonder if I should simply abandon my plan and leave this place. Of course, I wouldn't return the three of them back to their beastly states—I would keep my word about allowing them to remain human.

But, yes, this whole excursion might well prove to be a waste of effort. Maybe it's time I abandoned it. In which case, all I could do is hope for the best against Morningstar.

Deep down inside me, however, I know Beacon is right. None of them had any choice as soldiers of Kronos. If they refused to obey Kronos's bidding, it was a death sentence not only to them but also to everyone they cherished and loved.

So far, it seems the only one who has any interest in helping me is Alder, but that could simply be temporary and who knows if he'll follow through. No, I'm definitely of the mind that in order to get one of them to agree to help, I need to get all three of them to agree. And, certainly, Beacon is doing anything but agreeing.

My thoughts turn toward Horatius as I wonder if he'll prove to be as difficult as is Beacon.

Chapter Seven
Horatius

I hear Belle's light footsteps as she enters the garden.

Soon thereafter, I can feel her watching me.

I'm testing out my newly regained powers by controlling a cardinal overhead. I urge the creature down to the fountain before sending it back up mid-flight, moving the action in a continuous time loop. I make no attempt to acknowledge Belle, but I simply wait to see what she might say, because I'm fairly sure she doesn't know I possess such abilities.

"Fair morning," she finally remarks, going for casual but not quite arriving there.

"And the same to you," I reply, my eyes still fastened on the cardinal. "To what do I owe this visit?"

She scoffs. "I would think it's obvious."

I look back at her. "It's not."

"Well, if you recall, Prince Alder made it obvious that he wanted vengeance against me, something which I offered to all three of you," she answers on an impatient sigh. "So... What do *you* want from me?"

I shrug, I'm not interested in vengeance and never have been. "Only for my associates to be happy again," I say. "If you can manage that, I shall be perfectly content."

"What?" she scoffs, shaking her head so her long, black locks swish around her face as if she were underwater. She truly is a beautiful woman, though her beauty doesn't call to me the way it did to Alder. I could tell from the first moment he laid eyes on her that he desired her carnally. Beacon and I are different—we don't think with our cocks.

"No thirst for revenge? No pound of flesh for you?"

It's my turn to scoff. The previous night she spent with Alder must be giving her distorted expectations of what Beacon and I desire from her. She's been too quick to lump all three of us into the same basket when none of us are at all alike.

I release the cardinal at last, allowing it to fly far from this castle of sorrows in search of its freedom, something that has been denied me for the majority of my life. In much the same way, I often wish I could fly off like the cardinal, to leave the confines of my existence.

I note the bruises on Belle's body as I face her, unquestionably Alder's handiwork. Though I don't agree with Alder's way of handling the situation, I feel nothing towards her. I doubt Beacon has any desire to touch her, same as me.

"Beacon and I are not like Alder," I say with audible impatience.

"Then tell me what you are like," she retorts.

A slight grin curls my lips as I think of the easiest way to explain who and what I am before I begin to answer her implicit question. "I was bred for war."

"Go on."

"From the time I was old enough to walk, my life has been nothing but battle. But there was one lesson that was drilled into my head more than all the others: *you must win until you finally lose.*"

"Hmm," she says and I can't tell whether or not she agrees with the sentiment.

"In that context, losing means there is no coming back," I continue. "So why should I seek revenge against you simply because you got the best of me in the end?" I shake my head as she frowns, clearly unaccustomed to the way I think. I'll admit, it is quite strange. "And me losing was bound to happen sooner or later. I had no more choice in the matter than I did about being born."

"Then you want nothing from me?"

I nod. "I want nothing from you."

She doesn't seem pleased about this. "Beacon said the same thing, more or less, only he was much angrier about it," she replies on a shrug and then noticing a large bruise on her forearm, she points at it and adds, "Alder obviously harbors a lot more anger towards me than either of you do."

"Alder is an angry sort."

She nods. "I can't understand how you manage to remain so apathetic to your fate."

"Don't confuse apathy with ambivalence," I correct her, shaking my head. "In a way, you saved me from a lonely death on the battlefield."

Her eyebrows reach for the ceiling. "I did?"

I nod. "In turning us all into beasts and confining us here, you stopped us from experiencing what was, most likely, an early death. Given my upbringing, I probably would have been dead by now or I'd be well on my way. The same goes for Beacon and Alder. Ironically, your curse indirectly gave me something I never had before: boon companions."

"Companions?"

"Alder and Beacon are the closest thing I've ever had to a true family."

"I… I don't know what to say to that," she honestly admits, and her expression reveals the fact that I've quite flustered her.

"No reply is necessary," I respond with a quick smile. "It's simply a fact, just as clear as the sun above us." I decide to test the bounds of her perception. "Do you have any inkling as to what I am?"

"I didn't fail to notice the little time loop you just used on that bird," she says, nodding as she studies me with interest. "So, whatever your powers, I know they're quite substantial."

I give her a chill smile. "You gleaned all that from my one little exercise with the cardinal?"

"Time loops are no simple matter," she answers, nodding. "And you haven't had access to your power in years," she continues, eyeing me narrowly. "It was dormant, owing to my curse. Seeing how easy it was for you to bring that power back, after all this time and so soon after being returned to your true self, tells me the time loop is only a tiny fraction of what you *can* do." I start to sense a slight fear from her, yet she steps forward as boldly as any soldier in battle. "It also tells me that I made the right choice by cursing you when I did—before you had the chance to use your magic against me."

I nod. "If it's any comfort to you, I believe you might actually be stronger than I am at this point in time."

"What makes you say that?"

"Because you've been using and growing your power for the past sixteen years. I haven't. Although we were both novices in our ability to control our magic back then, I'm certain I would have dispatched you had I been given the chance."

She smiles at me and there's a challenge in her eyes. "That's something we'll never know for sure."

"Oh, I'm quite sure." I draw myself up to my full height and enjoy the fact that I tower over her. She's a small woman and I'm a large man—not quite so tall as Alder, but I'm broader. "You see before you no lowly hedge magician who can be defeated by mere brute force."

"So, what are you, then?"

I smile, long and languid. "I'm the son of Kronos."

"Kronos!"

I nod again. "I'm the tainted fruit of my mother's loins after she was raped by my father."

She gasps, obviously unprepared for such a revelation. "That's not possible," she says, swallowing hard as that shocked expression doesn't leave her face.

"You, of all people, should have a better grasp of what is possible," I chide her. "Like any tyrant, Kronos is obsessed with his legacy. That certainly includes all worthy heirs that he can manipulate as instruments of his will. He forced himself upon dozens of women, but only my mother gave him what he truly desired… a male child."

"And he made you serve him?" she asks, shaking her head as though trying to decide if she should attempt to understand me or run as far away from this place as it's possible to go.

"Yes, he did," I answer as thoughts of my father begin to plague me and my hands turn into fists at my side. I hate him. I always have. "Now, I believe I can rival Kronos' power, given enough time; but back then, I had little choice in the matter."

"Then… you never cared for him?"

"He was never a father to me," I answer with a shrug. "And I was never his son, merely a useful tool." A familiar cramp tugs at my heart as I add, "The time I've spent here, locked to these castle grounds, allowed me to realize you were never my enemy, Belle Tenebris. *He was.* He destroyed my life as well as all the lives he forced me to take in his name."

"What about your mother?" Belle asks in a quiet voice. "What did he do to her?"

"Nothing. She and my half-sisters were spared as long as I fought by his side and carried his flag." The pain begins gnawing at me again, and I tighten my jaw. "And, out of love for them, that's exactly what I did, yet he killed them anyway." I grow quiet as I think of my mother and sisters.

"Kronos must be stopped," Belle replies, her eyes narrowed and her jaw tight. "Kronos helped Morningstar take Delerood. And I've no doubt they're planning to do something far worse."

At last, we come to the reason she returned and was so willing to degrade herself before us. "Forgetting the curse you made us endure for the past sixteen years, why should I help you now?"

"You wouldn't be helping me so much as you would be all the innocent people of Delerood, including your family."

"My family are deceased."

"Then fight for their memory."

I admire her powers of persuasion and the fire with which she burns, but I'm still unmoved. I hate war and I've no interest in returning to it. Not when I've experienced the taste of peace for so long. "I don't know that I will be of much use to you," I answer, shaking my head as my voice trails. "It's been a very long time since I had access to my magic and I imagine it will take much longer than you anticipate for my magical reserves to fully refill themselves."

"If you are Kronos' son, then yours is the only power that can rival his," she insists, her eyes imploring. "Without you, Horatius, our battle is dire."

I tap my chin and look at her with unveiled respect. "Yet you are a Chosen one."

"How… how did you know that?"

"Do you think we are so isolated out here that news doesn't reach us?" I ask on a chuckle. She doesn't respond. "Needless to say, I know what you are and I know you're in search of the other Chosen."

"We've assembled all but one of them."

I'm surprised she admits as much when I still haven't promised to help her and, thus, could still be considered her enemy. Maybe it was a show of good faith that she allowed me such information. "Nine of the Chosen… shouldn't all of you provide enough power to defeat Kronos?"

"The Chosen might be powerful, but you are

his son—you embody *his own power*. You could help us in ways… ways no one has even considered."

I nod because she's correct. "So, what happens if I refuse to cooperate?"

"Then it is as I said it would be—I will allow you your humanity, but I won't fully break the curse and your isolation will remain."

"Unless I broke the curse myself."

She pauses and breathes in deeply. "The curse is impenetrable, even for the son of Kronos." She releases her breath and stares up at me and for the first time, I wonder what it must be like to bed her. Was she submissive with Alder or did she put up a fight? And how would she be with me? Would she fight me or would she allow me to worship her body, as a woman's body is meant to be treated? I have no doubt that seeing her naked would be a thrill unlike any other and strangely enough, I've felt myself warming to her in the time we've had this conversation. But I would never force her to my bed.

"If you refuse to help me, I'll still appeal to Alder and Beacon in order to secure their assistance."

"Even if you're ultimately destined to lose against Kronos and Morningstar as a result?"

She shrugs. "Perhaps all we need is the element of surprise. And maybe that's all you need to overcome Kronos, as well."

"That's still very iffy," I point out, shaking my head. When her expression falls, I hastily add, "I'm not refusing you. I'm just not ready to give you my consent."

"What would drive you to agree?"

"I know not. I suppose the answer will come to me when it comes."

"Then I suppose I'll just have to wait."

"What did you promise Beacon?" I ask, curious.

"To help him find his sister."

"And what about Alder?" I ask, even though I know the answer. For some reason, though, I want to hear the words from her lips. "What price did you pay to him?"

She pulls up her blouse to show the ugly purple and red bruises and welts he left on her lower back, no doubt with his whip he's so fond of carrying. "He got his pound of flesh from me last night." She pulls her blouse down and her jaw is tight.

"And he asked for nothing more?"

"I'm certain he *will* ask for something more, but as far as I'm concerned and as far as my agreement with him is concerned, I've paid my debt."

"And Beacon? Did he not demand to know you carnally? Intimately?"

She shakes her head. "Beacon pointedly said he wasn't interested in me."

I chuckle at that because she's less intelligent

than I give her credit for if she believes such toss. There is no way any man could look upon her and not feel attracted to her. She is undeniably beautiful. Yes, anger and hatred has a way of coloring attraction but the attraction is still there.

I feel it and there's something about the way she looks at me that makes me believe she feels it too.

Chapter Eight
Belle

After sundown, I retire to one of the vacant rooms of the castle.

No, I haven't been invited to stay, but I'm not going to leave until I get a response from all three men as to whether or not they're going to help me against Morningstar. So far, Alder seems to have agreed while Beacon refused and Horatius seems to be siding with Beacon. This isn't at all what I wanted and when I awake in the morning, I'm even more determined to align them with my cause.

I feel much better and my body is much less sore (from the treatment at Alder's hands) when I awaken at sunrise. After taking a moment to refresh myself, I dress as the scent of breakfast wafts in from under the door.

Making my way to the kitchen, I find Beacon standing over a large, cast-iron stove, cooking something I assumed he's caught—rabbit perhaps. My stomach begins to audibly growl and I can feel my cheeks redden with my embarrassment.

"Breakfast nearly done?" Horatius asks as he appears from the hallway. He doesn't even bother looking at me, but faces Beacon, who's still busy at the stove.

"Come see for yourself," Beacon replies as Horatius does just that. Meanwhile, Alder plops himself into the chair on my right and looks up at me with a leer.

"You're still here?" he asks.

I take a deep breath and nod. "I'm here until you make up your minds as to whether or not you're going to help me or… if you're going to instead choose to remain encased in this prison… forever."

"I want out," Alder replies as he looks to the other two. "I don't want to spend another bloody night trapped in this godforsaken, fucking place a second longer than I have to."

"That's you," Beacon answers. Then he glances over his shoulder and notices me, where I stand in the corner of the kitchen. "Well, are you going to sit?" he asks with no amount of kindness.

I've made no motion to join them because I'm not one of their guests—I know how they feel about and towards me. But I do hope the time has come for them to announce whether or not they've sided with me. Regardless, I need to leave this place soon.

Horatius and Alder return to the table with their plates in hand.

"I didn't realize I was considered a guest," I respond in a soft voice.

"Well, you're in this house, aren't you?" Horatius replies, raising his brows at me. "I'm sure you're hungry, woman."

I give them both a silent and grateful smile and help myself to a small plate, before returning to the table where I take a seat beside Beacon, who continues to study the food in front of him.

"So, what have you both decided?" Alder demands of his two friends.

No one responds as we settle into our aromatic meal. Maybe a few seconds later, Horatius says, "Yesterday, I made the choice to join Belle in her effort to stop Kronos and Morningstar's campaign to exterminate and imprison our people."

Beacon scoffs, but says nothing. Clearly, he's upset with Horatius' decision.

Horatius swallows his mouthful. "I also had to consider the price I want to extract from Belle in exchange."

I look at him in question because the day prior he had told me he wanted nothing from me. "You've changed your mind, then?" I ask.

Alder grins at him while Beacon frowns. "After what she did to us, how can you be so willing to help her?" the latter asks.

"*She* has nothing to do with it," Horatius starts, shrugging as he piles a huge bite into his mouth and then grows silent as he chews it.

"Might I remind you all that I'm sitting right here?" I interrupt. "Please stop calling me 'she'."

No one seems to care because they don't comment—they don't even look at me.

"We are required to assist by a higher authority," Horatius replies as soon as he empties his mouth. Then he turns to face Beacon. "Why haven't we heard from you regarding your stance on the matter?"

Beacon lifts his half-finished plate of food and stands up, shaking his head. "I'm not agreeing to it."

"The alternative," Alder starts, frowning.

"I know what the alternative is," Beacon interrupts, glaring at his friend. "And I actually prefer to stay here, and even go on being a monster, if I must."

Horatius catches his wrist and grabs it. "Beacon, stop for a minute and listen." Beacon stiffens a little but heeds his comrade. "Either we help Belle stop Kronos and Morningstar," Horatius explains, "or there will be nothing left of Delerood or any other place in Fantasia… including your sister."

"As if she's even still alive," Beacon argues.

"You don't know for sure what's become of Blaze," Alder argues. "She could have survived."

"The chances are few and far between," Beacon mumbles.

"If Morningstar isn't defeated, then all of Fantasia will crumble," Alder announces.

"How did that become our problem?" Beacon

growls.

"Because Morningstar won't be content to stop at one settlement," I tell him slowly. "He'll stay on the warpath until there's nothing left to seize and conquer."

"He wants all of Fantasia," Alder adds with a nod.

"And how long do you suppose it will be before he comes here?" I continue as I spear Beacon with an angry look. Of the three of them, I'd assumed he would be the easiest to win to my side. How wrong I was. "You'll be all alone here against his entire army."

Beacon jerks his hand away and leans against one of the stone walls. Holding his plate in front of him, he shovels in the rest of his food as if he no longer enjoys the taste of it. Horatius releases a long-suffering, audible sigh.

"You become downright unpleasant when you act like a spoilt child, Beacon."

"I don't trust her," Beacon snaps back, glaring at me.

"Neither do any of us," Alder says with a shrug, as if that's the accepted status quo.

"We all have our private reasons to end Morningstar's tyranny. None of them need to involve Belle. She's merely the means to our end. Is that not enough?" Horatius asks them both.

Beacon and Alder are silent for a moment, contemplating Horatius's point. Then Beacon says,

"Fine, I'll agree to help, but only if her powers are limited and contained—the last thing I want to experience again is her magic."

"Limited and contained?!" I repeat, ready to protest. Being subjected to their flippant whims is bad enough. Relying on the mercy of the world outside these walls will be far worse.

"I must agree with Beacon," Horatius says as he nods and faces me. "None of us want to be subjected to another of your curses—and that was the price I was going to say I wanted from you in return for my obedience to your cause."

"I've given you my word," I start, shaking my head.

"And your word means nothing," Alder interrupts.

"Why would I curse you if you're on my side?" I continue, thinking this is a huge mistake. Without my magic, I won't be able to defend myself. And they'd be fools to think we won't encounter enemies along the way.

"Not one of us trusts you, which means, in our eyes, you're a walking threat. Take away your magic and we take away the threat," Alder answers and gives me a grin that I want to smack off his smug face.

"We will agree to help you but in return, you'll agree to wear a locket of my design that suppresses your powers without affecting your physical strength," Horatius says, looking at Alder and

Beacon, who nod back at him. "That means you will possess little more power than that of a skilled human."

"What if we're attacked?" I postulate, glaring at all three of them in turn. "You think we won't encounter obstacles? Or that we won't encounter those who are loyal to Morningstar?"

"We can handle any attacks," Alder replies smugly. "In case you've forgotten, you'll be traveling with three able-bodied soldiers."

"Is that what happened when I cursed you all the first time?" I shoot back. "You *handled* the attack?"

He glowers at me. "Exactly the reason why we won't make the same mistake twice."

"If we need your powers for whatever reason," Beacon assures me, "we can release them quickly enough by removing the necklace."

I take a moment to glare at him icily. "I'm not so sure we share the same idea as to how quickly we can be overtaken and defeated. I'm not the only person out there who possesses magic."

"Horatius possesses magic," Beacon points out and Alder raises his brows as if to show he's surprised they've let me in on their secret. Not that I care—at the moment I'm too concerned with the impending loss of my own magic.

"Either it happens our way or the agreement is null and void," Horatius says quietly.

I scowl at him, but squelch my frustration. I

have even less reason to trust them than they do me. But if this is the only way I can get them to fight for Delerood and for the Guild, I have to take my chances. "All right, I'll do it," I reply.

"Then the deal is done," Alder smirks before continuing his breakfast.

My food sits cold and untouched before me.

###

I feel the plain silver amulet between my breasts as we prepare for our trip to Delerood.

I can sense my power being drained, like an open wound empties blood from a vein. As Horatius promised, I don't feel any weaker physically, but it's been a long time since I felt so powerless. I pray to the gods and goddesses that I don't regret my decision.

We decide to begin our journey as soon as night falls to ensure we travel undetected. I fling my pack strap across my shoulder and step outside the castle gates to watch the sun setting as I hope I can trust these three. There is definitely a chance they turn against me and with my missing magic, I'll be no better than a sitting duck. But I need them. Horatius especially—given the fact that he's Kronos' son. So, I suppose desperate times call for desperate measures.

"It is unfortunate that we must leave this place of sanctuary," Horatius says quietly as he appears beside me. I didn't hear him walk up, I was so caught up in my own frantic thoughts. When I look over at him, I realize he's referring to the serenity of our surroundings. And he's quite right—Castle Chimera is located in a beautiful place.

"I'd expect you to be more than happy to put it behind you," I reply with obvious surprise.

He shrugs. "In some ways, yes, it will be a great relief to leave the castle well behind me. But I will miss the beautiful, tranquil sunsets. And the landscape on which we stand. I shall also sorely miss my nightly ritual of climbing the tower at sunset and seeing everything for miles around. It's so peaceful there."

I look at him and wonder. "I never expected you to find contentment here."

"Regardless of your intentions," he answers, his tone going sour. "I found my own serenity nonetheless."

"What about Alder and Beacon?"

A low, knowing chuckle bubbles out of his throat. "Them? Not so much. Alder hated his monstrous form and the way he always repulsed anyone who ventured too close to the castle. Beacon, on the other hand, just fell into a never-ending cycle of simply existing."

"But you didn't have such a reaction?"

"I did at first. But once the initial horror passed, I realized it was a blessing in disguise. I finally had the closest thing to a family, I answered to no one, and, as I stated before, I was surrounded by the most marvelous views of the landscape."

"You embraced the curse and your exile."

"Fighting it was an endless exercise in futility," he answers with a clipped nod. "Besides, our life here is peaceful. No battles to wage, and very few visitors. The outside world could no longer touch us." He sighs. "But all things must come to end, even the most pleasant idylls."

The sound of horses comes from behind us and we turn to see Beacon and Alder leading four of the large animals, one of which is the horse I rode in on.

I turn back to face Horatius, who shrugs as he adds, "Who knows? Perhaps when this is all over, I shall come back here to live out my remaining years in the precious company of those sunsets."

The sun is nearly below the horizon. "I sincerely hope you get that chance."

Chapter Nine
Alder

I'm awakened in the middle of the night by the witch's screams.

Glancing over, I realize she's caught in a dream or nightmare as she thrashes about wildly. An owl in the tree above her calls a warning before taking flight and disappearing into the dark night sky.

"Wake up," I tell her, while shaking her out of the bad dream she's having. Usually, I wouldn't give a damn and I'd even encourage her to have a fitful night of sleep, but only if she were in her own room where her cries wouldn't awaken me. It's a damn wonder she hasn't also awoken Horatius and Beacon. But those two sleep like the damned dead.

"Bloody hell, will you wake up?" I say more loudly as she continues to toss and turn, making one hell of a ruckus.

She jumps with a start and snaps awake, a look of wild-eyed confusion on her face as she takes in the forest of branches above her and beyond those, the sparkling stars overhead. Taking a moment to look around, she apparently realizes where she is, in the middle of the Enchanted Forest, and settles down. Then she gives me a quick nod of apology before rolling over onto her side, putting her back to me.

And that's when I realize my cock is hard and I know just where I want to put it—immediately, memories of her tight wetness revisit me and I imagine pushing her against the nearest tree and thrusting into her as hard as I can.

Rolling closer towards her, I grip her waist and pull her against me so she can feel what I have to offer her.

"Get off me," she growls over her shoulder, giving me an angry expression to go along with her abrupt words. "I've already repaid my debt to you."

"I don't recall saying my debt should last the extent of one evening."

"Well, you didn't specify, did you?" she demands as she pulls away from me and sits all the way up. Even in the darkness of the night, I can see her scowl. She's beautiful, and it's that beauty that heats my anger. She has no right to be as lovely as she is. Not after what she did to us.

"*Neither* of us specified," I answer.

"Thus, as far as I'm concerned, that payback only lasted one evening." She gives me another glare and then lays back down, resting her head on her pack again, scooting her body forward so she's no longer in contact with mine.

"That's it then?" I inquire, trying to avoid

letting her know how annoyed she's making me. "You have a nightmare that puts the fear of the nine hells into me and then you turn your back on me?"

"That's it."

"What am I to do with this erection, then?"

"Try using it to dig for oil for all I care," she answers. "Or perhaps it would make a nice sturdy branch for that owl overhead." With that, she snickers.

"Blasphemous!"

"How in the world did you ever become a prince?" she snaps back, turning to face me and sounding like a shrewish wife. "I've met street-raised urchins with better manners than you have."

"Well, perhaps you'll remember that I also spent *the past sixteen years* as a fucking chimera and last I checked, those with three heads don't exactly give a fuck about manners and propriety!"

She continues to frown at me, but I'm fairly sure the ends of her lips turn up in a bit of a smile. "Are you saying it's my fault *you're* an asshole?"

"That's about right," I reply, doing my best not to feel even more turned on by our verbal sparring. I won't admit how long it's been since a woman dared to challenge me like this. It feels strangely… good and my erection feels even heavier than it did before. Damn her.

"No," she says, shaking her head. "You were an asshole long before you stumbled across me."

"Regardless, I still have a problem to address."

"And what problem is that?"

I reach inside my pants and cradle my enormous cock, which requires attention. Knowing it will upset her, but not caring, I pull my manhood from my trousers and begin stroking it right in front of her.

"I want nothing to do," she starts, but even as she says the words, her eyes immediately seek my erection and she watches me as I pleasure myself. I smile as she swallows hard, and it's all I can do to keep the memories of how wet she was for me, how ready, from my mind. Even though I was rough with her, she enjoyed it. She couldn't hide that from me. And even now I can see the way my erection has her captivated.

"Have you ever had a man's cock in your mouth?" I ask.

She looks at me and seems to remember herself because she instantly frowns, even with the blush creeping across her cheeks. "I don't care to sample yours, if that's why you're asking."

"Yet I can see the interest in your eyes." I chuckle as I continue to stroke myself, and a bead of wetness emerges from my tip.

"You disgust me," she spits the words.

"Maybe that's so, but you want me and you hate yourself for wanting me."

Her eyes narrow, but I can see the truth of my words in her gaze. "I… don't want you."

I quirk a brow at her that says I don't believe her for one moment. "Come, now, instead of fighting it, come closer."

She breathes in deeply and as I continue to pleasure myself, I can see the need clearly in her eyes. She wants to fight me, wants to fight the desire that, even now, is overcoming her.

"Why?" she asks. "What will you do to me?"

"Nothing," I answer as I pull down on my cock all the way to the base so she can see how fully engorged it is. How ready for her.

"Nothing?" she doesn't seem to understand my answer.

I shrug. "I will simply continue to sit here and you're going to sit on top of me."

"I am?"

I nod. "And you're going to take the whole length of my cock all the way inside your tight, and wet little pussy and you're going to ride me until you achieve orgasm."

She doesn't say anything for a few seconds, but nervously looks towards Horatius and Beacon, who are loudly snoring and completely lost to the moment. She turns to face me again and I chuckle.

"Make a decision soon, because I won't last much longer."

With that, she stands up and, much to my surprise, walks over to me. Throwing one leg over me, she straddles me and then stares me in the eyes as she lowers herself over me until I can feel her hot opening on the tip of my cock. I release my erection to place my hands on either side of her waist and as we both stare into each other's eyes, I pull her down on top of me, feeling my engorged cock stretching the walls of her silken channel.

As soon as I enter her, she throws her head back and moans. Then once I'm fully seated inside her, she begins to rock her hips back and forth.

"That's it, just like that," I whisper into her neck as she increases her momentum. "Use me for your own pleasure."

She grips my shoulders as she arches against me and I can feel the inside of her pulsing in time with her orgasm. Gripping her arms, I lift her slightly and then pound myself into her repeatedly, holding her in place while I thrust in and out of her tight little orifice. After another few seconds, I explode my seed inside of her and then pull away, exhausted and well-spent.

"That will be the last time I give myself to you," she says, once she catches her breath.

I chuckle in response and that seems to further anger her. "Whatever this is," she continues. "It's momentary and fleeting because the truth of the matter is that I can't stand you."

For some reason, her words cut me to the quick.

"And why is that? Shouldn't it be me who can't stand you?"

"I don't care what you think of me," she spits

out.

If she insists on being brutally honest with me, maybe hearing my side of the story will change her perception. "I wasn't always so hateful," I say on a shrug as I lean back on my bedroll and stare up at the branches overhead. It's still dark and the owl she so nicely mentioned earlier sits within the tree, calling out his doleful tones.

"I've heard that before," she answers on a yawn.

"I can promise you you haven't heard my story before."

She breathes in deeply then shakes her head. "Well, clearly, you aren't going to allow me to my slumber so go on, tell me."

"Everything I loved and cherished was ripped from me in a single day. One moment, I was happily enjoying my life, feasting at a banquet with my kin. The next moment, my family lay dead at my feet. I was the only survivor." I give her a hard stare as I add, "I'm entitled to be bitter."

"We've all experienced heartbreaking loss," she says, her unimpressed stare matching mine. "But not all of us subsequently endow that heartbreak with the power to render us bitter cynics."

"Yes, well, some of us have more reasons than others to be bitter."

"True enough, but we all have a choice in how we react to it."

"I had no choice."

"You *always* have a choice," she responds, shaking her head. "Everything we do in life is a choice we make."

I want to tell her that she doesn't know what she's talking about, but I don't because I can't argue the fact that she's serving up some pretty hard truths to accept, but she isn't wrong. I look at her and I see her eyes shining with intelligence and power. I also have to admit she has a pretty face. Her delicious body served me well as an excellent fuck. But...

"What are you looking at?" she demands.

"You," I answer simply.

"Why?"

"Aren't I allowed to look at you?"

"No."

I chuckle even as I acknowledge to myself something I haven't fully identified yet—there's a part of me that's changing—a part of me that doesn't dislike her as intensely as I did. I hate knowing that someone who cursed me for so many years is beginning to appeal to me in other ways. But I'd be lying if I said I didn't find her compelling.

"You say little about yourself," I say.

She shrugs. "I figure the three of you hate me, so why would you want to know about me?"

"While that's true—we most certainly *do* hate you—is it not a good idea to get to know one's enemies?"

She looks at me and then shakes her head. "Go to sleep, Prince Alder."

I see the light go out in her eyes, and the slight hint of amusement fades as she turns her back to me once more in a sign that she wants to return to her slumber. A sense of unfamiliar regret crosses my mind.

Gods, what's happened to me?

The last thing I need is a temptress like Belle Tenebris to distract me.

Fucking her senseless was one thing, but now I've got a problem. Perhaps it's because she's the first piece of ass I've had in more than sixteen years, but I have to confess she's the best piece of ass I've... ever had? Is that possible?

No, perhaps my memory of all the other women before her is just too faded?

Regardless, this situation is not good for either of us, but worse for me. The more she dislikes me, the better off we both are. We can still keep our deal, but I'll leave it at that. I'm randy as ever, but I'm not a hopeless, lovesick brute chasing a piece of ass, no matter how beautiful she is.

Then why do I feel like such a shit now? I already know the answer—perhaps she is correct and my life as a chimera has turned me into an irrefutable asshole?

The hells with it! I'm not wasting anymore of my thoughts on the woman who trapped me inside a monstrous body and banished me to a remote castle. What's done is done. Now I have to live with it. Still, I can't stop thinking about that nightmare she had and what could have scared and bothered her so much, no matter how hard I try.

I'm still debating what to do next when I finally manage to fall into an agitated sleep. Starting with a few nightmares of my own, my mind replays the events that culminated into the ruination of my life.

I relive all the terrible scenes as if for the first time: the final feast with my family, their merciless destruction, the meal with Kronos when he told me to either help him or perish with the rest of my kin.

He managed to convince me at the meal's end.

Not long after that, I learned that Kronos had secretly concealed a potion in my food that made me agree to his terms.

Beacon and Horatius also joined him, but only for the sake of their families.

I wasn't as lucky. Kronos slaughtered my family, but all that did was remove some of his leverage with me. Such was why he had to put me under a spell.

Then along came Belle, who cursed me with a different spell, and locked me in a different kind of cage. I've been playing prisoner for so long now, I wonder if I can even remember what it's like to be free.

That thought makes me forget my nightmares

quickly, along with the heartache of my family's death. Soon, I'm back on the battlefield... the last battlefield I walked. I'm surrounded by the screams of men, women and children alike. Armed, unarmed: none of it matters anymore.

Submit to Kronos or perish. That's the only law here.

Blood splatters the streets and buildings as I charge my way through the city. Beacon and Horatius slay their fair share at my side.

Then, a flash of light hits my eyes and I'm inside a dark and dreary castle.

My body is now that of a hideous beast. I'm comprised of three animals: a lion's head, a fire-breathing goat's head that faces backwards, and a snake's head.

I can't even roar like a lion. I just grunt and growl.

On either side of me stands an ogre and a cyclops, whom I recognize as Beacon and Horatius. I'm filled with horror, but the state of my physical being is the least of that horror.

I hear the screams of all the people I killed in my head, growing louder by the moment. Soon, I'm jostled awake.

Dammit all!

I hoped I wouldn't hear those screams in my sleep once I regained my human form. But nothing changes. Is that part of the witch's spell? Or is it the side of me that will not be silenced, the side of me I was forced to ignore in my service to Kronos?

That's what I hate most about what the witch did to me, what *Belle* did to me—she lifted the enchantment woven by Kronos that had allowed me to fight without any conscience. And stripped bare as I've been all these years, I'm painfully aware of all the innocent lives I've taken.

Chapter Ten
Beacon

It's hard to tell which of us is more startled when Belle catches me with the music box that reflects dancing figures of light in the center of a clearing of trees. I've come here to be alone with my thoughts and the figures of light that bring me my only joy. The music box is the only relic from my life before the curse—a life that was filled with happiness.

She wasn't meant to follow me and I sorely wish she hadn't.

"What are you doing?" she asks, watching the figures waltz from tree trunk to tree trunk with unmasked fascination.

"Reliving my past," I answer on a shrug.

She approaches the reflections for a better look, being extra careful not to touch them, as if they're real and will shatter if she does even though they're nothing but reflections of light.

"It's beautiful."

"Yes," I agree wistfully, "and one of the last times I can remember being truly filled with joy."

She frowns as she walks over to me. "I overheard Horatius telling Alder how much he enjoyed traveling with you both when you were soldiers… I imagine that time also brought you joy?"

I don't fail to notice how she grits her teeth when she mentions Alder's name. I've no doubt that whatever he did to her has left its mark. And, to be fair, I happened to roll over while in my sleep and witnessed the two of them deep in a sexual union and, by the looks of it, Belle was certainly enjoying herself. Thus, I wonder if her gritting her teeth at the mention of his name is more owing to her own anger towards herself, than him.

I have to admit that I found my own sort of curiosity as I watched them. Just as I've been cursed for sixteen years to the body of a cyclops, I haven't enjoyed the feel of a woman and I'm beginning to regret not taking Belle up on her offer of her body. Of course, it's not within me to take something from a woman that she wouldn't willingly want to give. And while that might be the nature of the situation between Alder and she, it's clearly not that way any longer. From what I witnessed the previous evening, Belle wanted everything Alder gave her.

I find myself envious.

"I did enjoy those times, yes," I reply, "but they were not the same as… other times, earlier times."

I return my stare to the figures at the ball, ignoring my irritation at her unexpected intrusion. This is a private moment which I almost consider sacred.

I'm startled when she reaches for my hand and holds it as we watch the figures together in silence. I don't pull away because I strangely feel a sense of calm by her presence. And that makes no sense at all, considering my calm was stripped from me by this exact woman sixteen years ago.

She asks me about my family, and I oblige her. As we watch the glowing, dancing figures together, I relay fond tales of growing up and the antics my siblings and I used to indulge in together.

In turn, she shares some of her own family history, telling me about her beloved sister and father, and some of the stories of their lives. My heart softens as she speaks so intimately about a family she clearly loves as much as I loved my own. She suffers every day for the loss of her father and sister just as dearly as I suffer my own losses. And underneath the sense of sorrow I feel for her is the realization that I could be one of the reasons she has no hope of ever seeing her family again.

That is a truth that is very bitter for me to face.

By the time we finish sharing our tales, the music box has stopped. The figures fade away into the dark nothingness of the Enchanted Forest, leaving only us in the darkness of the clearing, surrounded on all sides by the trees.

"I feel I've misjudged you, Beacon," she tells me.

"How is that?"

She cocks her head to the side. "You and I aren't so different. Each of us were just doing our best to protect our families."

"And we failed," I add, feeling a strange yet warm connection to her.

"And yet we keep going," she whispers. "Always seeking something that might ease our pain and soothe our sorrow."

I stare deeply into her eyes before releasing my hand. Whatever moment we just shared, it's not enough to cancel the years and years of loneliness and worry for my family that's plagued me. And regardless of her own suffering, this woman is the reason for mine.

Belle
One Day Later

At dawn, I hear a knock on the door.

"Time to get going," Alder calls from the other side. The night before, we were lucky enough to come across an inn, in which we ate and drank our fill and then retired, each of us to our own rooms. And this night, I stuck to mine.

As to what happened the other evening

between Alder and me, when I crawled into his lap and rutted him as though I were a common whore… it's a memory I could do without but one that continuously plagues me. I don't know what it is about that man, but no matter how much my mind might tell me he's nothing more than an onerous lech, my body continues to desire him.

And that is beyond frustrating.

"We've already stayed here too long." I hear Beacon's voice and imagine they stand side by side, both awaiting me.

I open the door and give them each a quick nod of greeting, not missing the fact that Alder's eyes immediately travel from mine to my breasts and then down further still, before he returns his gaze to mine and gives me a little wink that does nothing but infuriate me.

The man is insufferable!

By the time we reach the stable, Horatius has finished preparing our horses and packing the saddle bags with our provisions for the next leg of our journey. I am quick to mount my mottled brown and white mare and as I turn her around, I notice Alder stealing glances at the locket Horatius hung on my neck, removable only by them.

I'm not thrilled about having my powers hobbled. I feel out of sorts, as if I've lost a limb. But it's a small inconvenience compared to the horrible curse these three endured for sixteen years—a curse at my hands. At least I know my handicap isn't permanent or without any hope of reprieve. Anyway, my comfort zone is irrelevant when compared to saving Fantasia.

Along the route, my companions begin to relax. In a matter of hours, Beacon and Horatius begin regaling me with tales of their exploits prior to my curse. Mostly, they reveal the robust, resilient friendship between the two of them. They both express their delight in fighting together, but I also sense the deep regret they have regarding the side for which they fought. They don't talk about Kronos much or the lives they took in his name. Instead, they talk of times they spent together—the happy, joyful times.

Some of their ribald stories are so ridiculous, I believe they must be fictional. But what strikes me as bizarre is the envy I feel towards them, envy of their relationship. But why should I be jealous of them? Perhaps because all of their tales sound much more joyful than any of my own adventures.

If Horatius and Beacon aren't shy about their dalliances, Alder is another story. He doesn't say one word during their exchanges. And his silence surprises me.

I would expect him to be the most vocal when it comes to recounting conquests of any sort. Yet he says very little, barely grunting a few words as Horatius tells a story that's mostly about him.

In this story, Horatius describes a giant who kept several slave women to service him alone.

Alder was the protagonist of the tale and credited with cuckolding the giant. The story soon unravels into a macabre comedy of errors. After the three managed to kill the giant, they proceeded to enjoy the services of the entire harem. In the end, the harem women inherited the giant's castle and went on to become independent women of impressive means. I find myself laughing at the twisted tale, no matter how grim it sounds in places. The ugly aspects aside, it certainly amuses me.

And I have to admit, the idea of a harem of men does somehow appeal to me. The truth of the matter is that the longer I spend with them, the more I begin to admire each of the men. It's easy where Horatius and Beacon are concerned because they're both gentlemen but even Alder is growing on me, in his own way.

It's strange, to be sure.

Contrary to what I expected on this trip, I find myself becoming more drawn to this trio by the mile. I have to remind myself that these men are indirectly responsible for the massacre of my family. To like any of them, much less *all* of them, is an unforgivable insult to the memory of my kin. This inner conflict makes me wonder if my feelings towards these men, which make no sense to me but are nonetheless there, are even valid.

I'm more than relieved when we stop for a bit as I hope to find my chance to collect my thoughts and analyze them.

As the men set up camp in a field of daisies, I tell them, "I'm going to find a quiet place to myself."

"Oh? Must you seek respite from us?" Horatius teases.

"There is no sanctuary secure enough," I retort with a smile, picking up a blanket as I head for a small, meandering path in between the trees. It's a path cut by animals, not humans. "I just need a little peace and quiet to myself," I call over my shoulder. "I won't be gone long."

I make my way through the woods until I find a clearing where I spread a blanket across the ground and sit upon it cross-legged. Folding my hands neatly into my lap, I close my eyes, softly reciting the precious words I was taught long ago by my father. I can still hear his soothing voice in these moments. Losing myself in the rhythm of my mantra, I begin my meditation. When I'm finished, I'll try to cast a mild cleansing spell. However, I don't expect to be able to do much with Horatius's locket hanging on my neck, a locket I'm unable to remove.

I know because I've tried.

The sound of heavy boots crunching on the ground comes from my right and instantly distracts me. One of my companions must have come to observe or guard me, no doubt. If he remains silent and allows me to have my peace, he can stay. It's comforting to know they're actually concerned about my safety.

All at once, though, I find myself being yanked up before a heavy arm slides around my waist and a knife tip presses into my neck.

I start to scream, but the blade digs into my skin, cutting off any sound I want to make.

"Make any noise an' it'll be the last sound ye ever make, lass," a familiar voice snarls from behind me.

"Gatz!" I whisper tightly as my heart drops down to my toes.

"Aye, lass, an' aren't ye delighted to see me, me lovely?"

Delighted? No. Quite the contrary, but I won't allow him to think I'm scared.

"Well, I can't actually see you when you're behind me, can I?" I spit the words at him.

Gatz laughs. "True, true… but we'll fix that soon enough, we will."

"I'm not alone," I say calmly. "My companions will come for you."

"Oh? I think not. They're too busy settin' up camp. By the time they realize you havenae returned, ye an' I will be long gone."

"I'm not going anywhere with you," I tell him, my stomach churning with dread. Of all the times to be caught powerless!

"Aye, ye are, Belle. You're comin' with me, an' soon you'll be servicin' me every urge before I turn ye over to Kronos."

"And if I refuse?" I counter. "Will you kill me?" I breathe in deeply and shake my head. "Might as well save us both the time and just do it now."

"Why should I obey any request from you!? There are plenty who cannae wait to do far worse things to you. Morningstar an' Kronos will be more than happy to make ye wish for death, which would be a kindness an' mercy. So, cross me once an' I'll hand ye straight over to them!"

The knife goes deep enough into my neck to draw blood.

Chapter Eleven
Alder

"She's been gone a long time," I comment to the others as we finish setting up the camp.

"Looks who's concerned about a wench he bedded," Beacon teases.

"You speak as though you're immune to her charms," I snap, trying to mask my uneasiness, but it won't go away. Beacon simply frowns at me and I take his frown to mean that Belle certainly has gotten under his skin, just as she has mine. "Something's wrong. She should have been back by now."

"You seem quite paranoid this morning." Beacon replies.

Horatius rises from his seat at the campfire, his eyes narrowing like they always do when he's concerned. "No, Alder's right. Something's amiss, and we need to find out what."

Nodding at Horatius's good sense, I rise to my feet. "Beacon, you stay with the camp," I order, "and be ready for anything."

Beacon silently nods before he starts looking around the camp perimeter. Meanwhile, Horatius and I head down the path that weaves between the trees, which Belle followed. I mentally scold myself for letting her go off all alone. With her power extracted from Horatius' locket, she's vulnerable to any and all sorts of mayhem. One of us should have gone with her... but she'd asked for her privacy and we *are* camped in the middle of the Enchanted Forest, far from the dirt road bisecting it.

I thought she would be safe on her own, but when I spot her blanket in the clearing, alone and unattended, I realize how wrong I was. My heart immediately starts pounding as panic begins to wend its way through me. I have no time to stop and ponder why I even care so much.

"Someone's taken her," I say, my voice coming out angry and deep, more of a growl, really.

There's no sign of her, but I see small drops of fresh blood on the blanket and the sight causes my heartrate to triple. I also notice boot-prints that flatten the grass beside two parallel indentations in the ground that could only be made by feet being dragged. Both tracks disappear into the woods on the other side of the clearing. I struggle to contain my rage when Horatius dabs his finger into the blood.

Rubbing the blood between his finger and thumb, he says, "The blood is still warm. They've not been gone long."

Though I can't explain why, because the witch means nothing to me, my anger triggers my animal instincts to take over and I find myself on the trail of the tracks through the woods. Strangely enough, living as a chimera for so long leaves me with so many common impulses to the beast: the snake's silence, the goat's tenacity, and the lion's predatory skills. At the moment, I'm grateful to the witch for that small part of the curse being preserved—if that part of me is even owing to the curse—maybe it's simply become… me.

Why does it matter if she's been taken? I ask myself. *This is your chance to flee this place, with or without Horatius and Beacon, and live your life as a free man, a human.*

I realize with some irritation that it does matter that the witch, that *Belle*, has been taken. And I can't just leave—not when she could be coming to harm. And owing to the scene before me, I'm quite convinced she *is* coming to harm.

The disturbed thoughts flee my mind as I pick up the scent of the sweetness of her skin, and on the air I can taste the sharp tang of her blood. There's something more—the odor of sweat, of man. Thinking of the filthy man who must be with her causes me to see red. From what I can scent, whoever abducted her seems to be alone. Good! Makes it that much easier to tear the perpetrator limb from limb when I catch up to him.

Alder, what in the bloody hell has gotten into

you? Why do you care what's happened to her?

I can't answer my own questions because, suddenly, I hear a shrill yelp, followed by the sounds of struggle. Breaking through the heavy brush, I find a man lying on top of Belle, overpowering her, his hands on her breasts, and his crotch violently pummeling her, though his clothing is still intact. The sun reflects off the knife blade he holds above her as she does her best to fight him off, while also avoiding the blade he wields. I manage to get a good look at his face as he turns his head and my blood boils.

Gatz! Even in the depths of the ninth lowest hell, I'd know him anywhere.

At the sound of our approach, he turns around and, seeing the two of us, obviously decides this is a battle he wants no part of because he immediately jumps up and runs away, seeking shelter deep in the woods.

"I'll get Belle back to camp," I hear Horatius shouting at me. "You deal with him."

As if I need permission!

I plan to shred the would-be rapist when I catch up with him. But, before I can do what I need to, I turn to face Belle.

"Return my curse to me," I say.

Instantly, her eyebrows meet in the center of her face because she doesn't understand what I'm asking.

"The necklace," Horatius answers as he

immediately unfastens it from around her neck, because he does understand my intentions and he realizes she won't be able to access her magic with the necklace in place.

"Belle, turn me back into the chimera," I tell her again. She faces me with a quick nod and then closes her eyes, holding her hands up towards me. I feel her magic spinning around me, something akin to standing in the center of a tornado. An instant later, my lion nose detects Gatz' scent, and I sprint through the woods after him.

After a feverish pursuit, I catch sight of him crossing a clearing just before he disappears again. All of a sudden, his scent evaporates and in its place is the acrid smell of singed hair, cooked flesh and brimstone. And I know that scent… Fucking hellhounds are somewhere near! Did that idiot Gatz summon them here? The answer becomes quite obvious as the hellish beasts suddenly flank me in either direction as I break through the trees into the clearing. I find myself standing in the center of the clearing with the nasty beasts surrounding me from all sides. I've got a much bigger fight now than I bargained for.

So be it.

Someone has to keep these bastards away from the others.

Unexpectedly, a massive blast of air hits me.

The trees behind me instantly combust into flames and a woman appears between them, attempting to get behind me with a short sword in her hand. Though she is decidedly attractive with her brilliant red hair and ice-blue eyes, I'm fairly sure she's trying to kill me.

I knock her off her feet with my paws when she hurls herself at me again. Throwing her off to the side once more, I glimpse a more serious dilemma. The hellhounds have come even closer, circling us both from all directions.

The woman gets on her feet and lobs another fireball, this time turning to face the tree line, clearly aiming the blaze at the beasts. The fireball ignites a huge fire that dwarfs the initial flames she set. In an instant, all the hellhounds come bounding out of the woods towards us, their fangs bared and their heads aflame. The fearful look they give as they pass this wild woman makes it plain she's no ally to them.

And, yet, I'm fairly sure she just tried to attack me, so perhaps she's lacking all her wits?

The only place to escape is behind us and we have no chance of fighting this many hellhounds. I grab the girl's hand with my large paw and run, hearing a beast snarl and whine behind me. She flicks her finger at the underbrush, creating a fiery barrier that prevents them from coming any closer.

I need to get that bastard, Gatz, soon, but maybe I'll be lucky and the hellhounds will eat him first.

###
Horatius

"What happened?" Beacon asks me as I walk Belle back to our camp.

"Gatz happened," I reply, doing my best to restrain my fury so I can think. "He was attempting to force himself on her before Alder tackled him."

"And where's Alder now?" Beacon asks as he follows me with a furrowed brow and tense jaw to a spread-out blanket.

"Sit and catch your breath," I say to her and she nods as she seats herself on the blanket and then pulls her knees up toward her chest, holding onto them while rocking slightly back and forth. It's strange to see her vulnerable like this when, up until now, she's displayed nothing but determination and strength.

Noting the blood that still drips from her throat as well as the numerous bruises that are already coloring her otherwise porcelain skin, I retrieve a healing crystal from my pouch and say, "I hope Alder is making Gatz beg for a quick death."

Beacon kneels down beside Belle, attempting to comfort her while I press the crystal against her head. Fairly soon, her entire body is encompassed by a soft white glow—a sign the crystal is working.

Beacon's eyes go from her to me. "Which way did they go?"

"They're most likely many miles away from us

by now," I tell him.

"I'll look for them anyway," he insists. "We must make sure Alder is okay. Which direction?"

I tilt my head roughly toward the direction of the clearing and Beacon takes off. I doubt there's anything he can do except assist Alder in his retaliation against Gatz, but at least I now have some time alone with Belle. My hope is that I can both calm and heal her and find out the extent of her injuries. I feel guilty for having taken her power away and disabling her from defending herself against the bastard.

"I," she begins, "I couldn't stop him…"

I breathe in deeply because I realize it's my fault she couldn't stop him. I should never have taken her magic away. "You're safe now and Alder will see to it that Gatz pays for what he did. Just breathe deeply."

She shakes her head, but her eyes are still distant and alarmed. "Much easier said than done."

"Here," I tell her, reaching for her hand and closing it gently around my own. She doesn't object, although I can feel her trembling as I hold her. The crystal in my other hand works its magic, brightening with each unsteady breath she takes.

"Deep breaths," I instruct her. "Then exhale slowly." I demonstrate the calming breaths until she matches her breathing with mine. Slowly, the crystal lightens and reveals its pure essence.

Just as slowly, Belle begins to focus on the

crystal. She frowns and asks, "What's that tingling sensation?" She tries to pull her hand away from mine, but I grasp it a bit tighter. She looks at me with renewed fright in her eyes.

"It's just the healing stone," I tell her, tapping the crystal with my free hand. "The cuts and bruises should be healed and gone by the time the tingling stops."

"Oh," she replies, relaxing again and returning to the breathing I coach her through. It helps her regain her composure more rapidly.

I've forgotten how it feels to do a calming ritual on a woman. Having employed it a number of times with my own sisters, I soon mastered the technique after Kronos terrorized them on a regular basis. I try to ignore the memory and the anxiety that always accompanies it.

"You seem lost to your thoughts," Belle says, bringing my thoughts back to the present.

"I'm just thinking of my family," I admit.

A guilty look appears in her eyes. "That's my fault—that I took you away from them."

I shake my head. "Admitting one's blame cannot change what happened."

"Perhaps you could have done more to save them if I hadn't cursed you."

"Perhaps I might have perished if you hadn't cursed me. Fate decides all things in the end." I give her a firm but gentle squeeze with my hand. "You can agonize for days over questions like those, but what's the point when you'll never come up with an answer? What's done is done. It's the here and now we must focus on."

Her eyes go from guilty to thoughtful. "I don't regret what I did to you or to Alder and Beacon," she says on a deep breath. "My intention was to save lives. You understand that, right?"

"As one soldier to another, yes, I do," I reply.

"I do regret, however, that I left you cursed for so long. I feel terrible about what it may have cost all of you," she goes on as she shakes her head. A tenderness creeps into her eyes. "I realize now that none of you are the monsters I thought you were."

"Perhaps we have all changed with time," I admit, though certainly I would never agree that we were monsters before—we were just subjects to an unfair destiny.

"What would have happened to me today if you and Alder hadn't come looking for me?" she asks, and some of the fear returns to her eyes. "You could have just as easily let me perish at Gatz' hands, thereby releasing yourselves of any further obligation to me or the guild."

"Knaves and cowards might choose that path," I say with some pride. "But Alder and I are neither."

"I can see that now," she replies with a small smile. "It's hard to admire your enemy's virtuous qualities in battle when they appear as faceless warriors who must be defeated." For the first time, she squeezes my hand. "But we're not enemies now... are we?"

I smile at her, feeling genuinely touched. I definitely don't consider her my enemy any longer. Truly, I never really did. I understood why she did what she did. And, had I been in her place, I would have done the same. War forces you to make difficult decisions.

I watch the bruises on her face start to heal and the long cut above her eye seals itself before fading away. In a matter of seconds, it vanishes completely, along with the other cuts and bruises that marred her lovely body.

"There," I say, letting go of her hand. "You're all better now."

I put the healing stone back in the small bag where I keep my other magical stones. I'll have to replenish its magic later, but only in a place where I'm guaranteed a good amount of time. It will take quite some time to replace all the energy I expended from the stone.

"Thank you," she replies. "For healing me."

"It was my honor."

"And... thank you for coming after me."

"Of course," I softly reply. "We promised to keep you safe." Feeling somewhat ashamed, I add on a sigh, "And today, we failed you."

"No, you didn't," she argues, shaking her head. "I should have known better than going off on my own. I just... I thought I'd be safe in the thick of the forest."

"As did we."

She's quiet for a moment. "Horatius, can I ask you something?"

I look at her and then nod. "Of course."

"Do you still… find yourself unattracted to me?"

I feel my eyebrows reach for the sky and surprise ricochets through me at her question, not to mention the fact that she even asks it at all—why does she care what I think? "You are a beautiful woman."

"But am I beautiful *to you*?"

It's then that I realize there's only one way to answer this question. I gently push her back onto the blanket. My previous reservations about her blow away like autumn leaves in a winter wind. There's nothing cold or wintry about her. Every inch of her healed body looks as warm and fresh as a sunny spring day.

I lean down and claim her lips with my own. She eagerly kisses me in response and then I pull away, tilting her head so her neck is open to me. Leaning down, I trail kisses down the front of her delicate throat, and she pushes my lips closer to her throat, which I interpret as her open invitation to pepper more kisses there.

"Suffice it to say," I start in a throaty voice, "Yes, you are beautiful to me."

Her subsequent moan makes my body quiver

with pleasure. She strokes my face as I look at her in undisguised awe. I kiss her again, and our tongues dance a lazy tango of raw desire and she pulls me even closer.

"Is it wrong, Horatius, that I… want more with you?" she asks as she pulls away and swallows hard.

"It's not wrong," I answer as I reach out and touch her breasts through her tunic. "Because I want more with you."

"Then take what you want from me," she whispers as she takes my hand and escorts it beneath her blouse so I can feel the warmth of her breasts. As I touch her, her nipples pebble.

"Can I," she starts and then loses her nerve.

"What?"

"Can I… taste you?"

She leans forward then and begins unbuttoning my trousers, releasing my engorged erection to the coolness of the air. When she sees it, she swallows hard and before I can say a word, leans down and takes my tip between her lips.

And the feel of her mouth is… exquisite. She opens her mouth fully and takes more of me inside her, sucking on me as she looks up at me and I watch her. Gods, the need to drive myself inside her is suddenly all consuming.

"Belle," I groan.

Suddenly, a loud explosion sounds through the otherwise still air, echoing against the trees. I leap to my feet as I struggle with the buttons of my trousers and both of us prepare for whatever fight is coming our way.

A load roar is audible in the distance, one which could only belong to Alder. What kind of trouble has my comrade gotten himself into?

Chapter Twelve
Blaze

I aim a small stream of fire downward, hoping to hit the creature's feet.

I'm still trying to figure out where this thing came from and what the bloody hell it is. Whatever it is, it's quite ugly with its three heads.

There were a pack of hellhounds chasing me for the last several miles when this creature came out of nowhere. Being quite the repulsive beast, at first I worried I'd have to add it to my list of attackers, but soon it became apparent the creature was being stalked by the hellhounds, just as I was.

Then, before I could blink, the creature (which I think might be a chimera) suddenly lifted me up and took off with me!

It's my own fault the beast abducted me—I should have been more aware of my surroundings. But I was so exhausted from trying to outrun Morningstar's horde and being slowed by the supplies in my pack didn't help either.

Well, let's see if a few little sparks do the trick.

I spray the creature with a round of fire sparks and the creature drops me off its shoulder and onto the ground as it yelps out its surprise. Instantly, I struggle to conjure up fresh flames in order to protect myself. As I form the fireball, the thing roars from his throat:

"I just rescued you and this is the thanks I get?!"

"What the hell are you?" I gasp, glaring at the thing. "You can speak."

All three of its heads appear surprised for a moment or two. "You can understand me?"

I glare at it. "Of course, I can understand you!" I take a deep breath. "What were you doing back there and why... why did you help me?"

"I was trailing a bastard named Gatz," the lion head responds. I'm fairly sure it's the leader. "I can only hope those hellhounds ate him."

"Not very likely," I tell him, snuffing out the fireball and picking myself up because I'm fairly sure the creature doesn't mean me any harm.

The baying of the hellhounds sounds closer as I ask, "Why go after Gatz?"

"He attacked a woman traveling with me," he explains, padding around to anticipate the pack's approach. Meanwhile, his other two heads sniff the air and his long, snake-like tail twitches.

"Hmm, and who is this woman?" I ask, wondering if she might need my protection against this... creature. I'm still not exactly sure if he's friend or foe.

"Her name is Belle."

"Belle Tenebris?" I repeat, eyeing him narrowly because such is the only Belle I've ever heard of.

"Why?" he asks, eyeing me just as narrowly.

"Is the woman you're traveling with one of the Chosen?" I continue as I realize if he's protecting one of the Chosen, maybe we are on the same side, after all.

He grunts his surprise. "You know her?"

"I know *of* her," I correct, but there's no more time for talk. The hooves of the hellhounds are fast approaching, closing the distance we barely managed to put between us.

"Come," the creature says and starts forward, but it's too late. The hounds have already reached us.

The fireball is easier to conjure this time, and I hurl it in their direction, hoping to catch them unawares. They have their own fire source, but my flames burn hotter than anything they can withstand and because my magic is different to theirs, my fire can still harm them—just as their flames can harm me.

A loud boom sounds as the trees blaze, their parched branches and leaves conducting the heat all around us like a burning cloak.

"Gods, everything is on fire!" the man-beast mutters, pushing me to one side.

"Did I get them then?" I ask hopefully.

"No, everything *but* them is on fire!"

That's when I hear the hounds nearer the flames. They yelp and wail in fear, but not one of them dares to cross the fiery barrier I've ignited between us. And that's definitely a good thing.

Abruptly, the chimera grabs me around my waist and, tossing me over his shoulder, says, "Hang on." Ordinarily, I would protest, but it's not in my best interest to complain at the moment—not when everything around us is ablaze and he's clearly trying to find a way out. He quickly scales a nearby tree only after reaching out to test the feel of it with one of his paws. I touch it and find it feels cool, so contrary to his statement, *not* everything is on fire.

Once we reach the top of the tree, the chimera begins swinging from branch to branch, gripping me tightly as his long tail does all the work of clinging to one branch and swinging to the next. His efforts put us further away from the burning forest. No matter how far we go, the scent of smoke remains. The fire keeps moving all around us. Gods, what have I done?

"Dammit, we're trapped," he says, dangling back and forth on a branch as he apparently tries to figure out what to do next.

"There's no escape?" I ask, my heartbeat starting to beat double-time. As I glance at the scene below us, it's nothing but flames and smoke.

"The flames are spreading around to the other side but, as you can see, we're still stuck in the middle. Those hellhounds will be burned alive, but so will we if we stay here."

I'm contemplating what to do when he adds, "You started this. Can you put it out too?"

"I don't know," I admit.

"What do you mean, you don't know?" he snaps impatiently. "You either can or you can't."

"Well, if I can, I don't know how to do it," I snap back, shrugging as I shake my head. I'm new to this magic business. "I'm still learning how to control my powers."

"For fuck's sake," he mutters in disgust. My irritation with him aside, I can't blame him too much. Sealing our fate by putting us in the middle of a blaze that burns hotter than any hellhound is a particularly stupid way to die.

That thought brings up another question, "Are the hellhounds still down there?"

"Uh-uh, they cut and ran before the fire got too big. But the route they took is burning, so we can't follow them."

"Hmm…"

All three of his heads glare at me, but it's the lion's mouth that speaks.

"Yeah, you really fucked this up," he growls, his words punctuated by a leap to another tree. "Just hang on, all right?" Even as he says the words, I can smell the smoke moving in from all sides, and I hear the leaves popping, and the tree sap sizzling. Everything around us continues to burn unabated. I brace myself for the moment when we get barbecued.

That's when a new sound joins the fire's crackle, a rhythmic pounding and hissing just ahead of us.

"What the hells is that?" the beast asks while continuing to swing to another tree limb.

"What do you see?" I ask because I can't see a damned thing.

"Steam," He answers. And that must mean water. I look beyond the smoke and what I see is a true shock—it appears to be a wave rolling in from the sea to douse the fire. Clearly, it's magic, but as to who's magic? I'm unsure. Under the roar of the wave, I barely make out the sound of feet crunching through the charred forest floor below. Two sets of footfalls, belonging to a man and woman.

When they grow close enough, the man-beast exclaims, "Belle!"

Then the oncoming rush of water overtakes us, sizzling the fire as it extinguishes it, leaving behind the acrid smell of wet, burnt wood. Both of us are soaking wet. Silence follows the wave's wake, and there are no more sounds of burning fire, but no animal sounds either. I hope the woodland creatures managed to escape rather than perish in my near-fatal miscalculation.

"Well, are you coming down, Alder?" the woman asks, whom I assume is Belle, though I've never seen her before.

"Damn right I am," the beast roars before beginning his slow climb down from our tree. Once at the bottom, he drops me on my feet in front of the pair that found us. The woman gives him a knowing smile and then closes her eyes, reaching her hands out to him and a second or so later, the creature is long gone and standing in its place is a very handsome man. And one who's completely naked.

"Is there a way you can gift us all our curse so we can rely on it when we need it?" he asks her and she shrugs, thinking about it.

"I don't see why not," she answers and then holds her hands out to him again as she mutters a few words. I can see white light begin to build from her hands and a moment later it disappears. When she opens her eyes, she smiles at him and in her eyes I can see the fact that this man means something to her.

"There, you're all cursed again," she says with a laugh. Then she turns to face me, as if only just realizing I'm standing there.

"Who is this?" she asks.

Taking a deep breath and trying to calm the frantic beating of my heart, I respond, "I'm Blaze."

"Nice to meet you, Blaze," she replies. "This is Horatius and you've already met Alder… the naked one," she adds with a laugh.

"That's one way of putting it," I reply wryly.

"Here, cover up that trouser snake with this, would you?" Horatius all but demands as he passes Alder his shirt.

"Seeing as you're so jealous of it…" Alder snipes back with friendly contempt.

Horatius shakes his head and then returns his gaze to me. "How did you meet this pretty one?"

"While I was tracking Gatz," Alder explains. "She came running toward me with a pack of hellhounds nipping at her heels. Imagine my surprise when she lobbed a fireball at the stupid bastards." He grunts and shifts his weight a little. "Of course, then she tried to fry my heels with a bit more fire."

"I thought you were planning on making me your dinner," I say to him indignantly.

"Fucking hell," Alder mutters. "Speaking of dinner, I'm bloody hungry."

"Well, it's lucky for the both of you that we came to see what that explosion was about," Horatius tells him.

"I had everything under…" Alder begins to say before heavy footsteps on the charred leaves and trees behind us cut him off. I turn toward the sound, poised for a new fight if necessary. The steps come to a stop, no more than a stone's throw away from me. And then I can't believe my own eyes…

"Blaze?" the man asks and I find I can't speak, can't even think for a few seconds. The shock of his all-too-familiar face stuns me into silence.

It can't be him! Not after all this time. I must be… imagining this.

"You know her?" Alder asks.

Beacon comes closer to me and before I can say a word, he throws his arms around me and lifts me off the ground. He holds me tightly against him as if I'm his most cherished possession. I do my best to return the hug, which is really quite smothering, his warmth and comfort spreading through my body.

"I can't believe you're here, Beacon." I breathe into his chest as tears burn my eyes.

"I'm here, Blaze, I'm here," he tells me in a soothing tone.

"How do the two of you know each other?" Belle asks. I'm sure Alder and Horatius have the same question on their minds.

Beacon finally pulls away, his hands still on my arms as tears bleed from his eyes. Tears that match my own.

"She's my sister," he tells them in a heavy voice.

"Well, I'll be damned," Alder grunts.

"Appropriate sentiment, given how everything reeks of hellfire right now," Horatius remarks. "Let's get back to our comparatively comfortable camp, shall we?"

Beacon finally lets go of me before taking my hand to guide me toward their encampment.

Beacon

"Tell me everything," I say to Blaze, offering her a glass of ale.

Even when she wraps her slim fingers around the glass, she doesn't look down towards it. Her eyes simply stare at me as if she's taking in every detail of my face, comparing it with her memory of me. How we even managed to recognize one another, I don't know. Sixteen years can certainly change a person, but it didn't change Blaze. I recognized her fiery red hair and those sky-blue eyes immediately. And I'm happy to see that the sparkle in her eyes hasn't faded one bit.

"Where would you like me to start, big brother?" Blaze answers after taking a sip of ale.

I clear my throat. "You're out here traveling alone?"

"I'm running an errand for the Guild, whom I serve."

"Serve?" I repeat, shaking my head. "The whole point of my servitude was so you would never have to—"

"And yet it happened," Blaze snaps, cutting me off. I feel shame in my gut and a flush of color fills my cheeks. She sighs and reaches out to me until she feels my hot cheeks.

"I'm sorry, Beacon."

"And what is Milady Blaze's business?" Alder chimes in. "Deforestation?"

I glare at him for his ill-tempered remark while she smoothly replies, "I'm simply a messenger. When the Guild needs to convey a message, they send me." A soft frown forms as she takes another sip and swallows. "Only problem is: the hellhounds never lost my scent. Everywhere I go, they always follow me. In fact, I think this is the first time I've been without them in a long while."

I put a hand on her shoulder. "I should have been there for you when they attacked. I will always regret that I wasn't."

"Hey, at least I was," Alder adds, but I ignore him. As does Blaze.

"Not sure it would have changed anything," she says, putting her hand atop mine. "We could have both died, thanks to those hellhounds."

"But we would have been together," I insist. "Not so far apart for years and years."

"Where have you been all this time, Beacon?" Blaze asks in a gentle tone.

Belle draws in a deep breath as she looks away; then she slowly exhales before repeating the cycle. She's, no doubt, willing herself to stay calm, or maybe she's worried that the truth will immediately turn Blaze against her. I don't want Blaze to turn against her because in the time I've spent with her, I've realized just how wonderful a woman Belle is. And I want my sister to see that as well.

"I was cursed," I explain. "Transformed into a *creature* that was confined to a castle for the last sixteen years. I have only now been released."

"Merciful gods!" Blaze reacts in horror, her mouth dropping open as a fresh spray of tears coat her eyes. "Who would do such a thing to you?"

"An opponent in battle," I say, avoiding all eye contact with Belle. When Alder accused me of having feelings for her, he was right. I do. But I also believe we all do.

Much to my surprise, Belle turns her head in our direction and addresses Blaze. "I was the one responsible for Beacon's curse—and that of Horatius and Alder."

"What?" Blaze asks, her voice sounding incredulous as her eyebrows knot in the middle of her face. "Why?" she shakes her head as if not understanding how that can be.

"They were trying to kill me," Belle goes on, her voice thickening with her burdensome guilt, "and those I loved. So, I did what I had to do. I've since released them from the curse and the castle."

"I'm afraid this doesn't make any sense," Blaze says. "First, you curse and isolate them. Now, these many years later, you're traveling with them?"

"We have an understanding," Belle replies, her eyes shifting around to the rest of us. "And, suffice it to say, but I believe we've... grown on each other."

"That's one way to put it," I laugh and give her a shy smile, one which she returns.

"Are you one of the Chosen?" Blaze asks her to which Belle nods.

"As am I," Blaze says.

When the full implications of those words sink in, I look at Blaze in confusion. "You're what?"

"I know it sounds crazy," she starts, shaking her head. "I just found out, myself."

Horatius just shrugs and says, "She can create fire magic. There's a certain verse in the Prophecy that foretells this."

For myself, I'm still too much in shock to fully comprehend her words and the meaning behind them.

"Too bad the Prophecy couldn't tell me how to keep my people from being killed," Belle adds ruefully. "That's why I freed your brother, Horatius and Alder, and lifted the curse, Blaze. I need their help."

"Ah," Blaze says as she nods. "War makes strange bedfellows, I suppose."

I say nothing in reply. How close to the truth her statement is!

Belle says, "No point in keeping secrets among us."

"That is beautiful music to my ears," Blaze says, nodding. "My life has been nothing but secrets for too long. I pass messages from this one to that one, often without even knowing what I'm conveying or to whom."

"So why do you continue to do it?" I ask.

A laugh bubbles out of my sister's throat. "What choice do I have? We're in a time of war and everyone must do her part."

"But you're not just any girl," Belle asserts. "You're the last of the ten Chosen." She shakes her head at my sister. "Even with fire magic, I'm not sure how you managed to survive so long… on your own."

Blaze shrugs. "I suppose I've learned how."

Alder stands up. "I've gotta go take a piss. Want to come hold it for me, Horatius? I get tired of doing all the heavy lifting myself."

"Would you two stop behaving like imbeciles?" I bark at them. "Need I remind you, there are two ladies present."

"Try not to set the woods on fire again before I get back," Alder mutters before disappearing into the trees nearby.

"Then try not to take too long," Blaze replies with a smile. "I get bored easily."

After Alder gives a final harrumph, Horatius and Belle fall into a quiet talk between themselves. I do the same with my sister, letting her lean on my chest as she used to do when we were younger. I'm beyond grateful to have her restored to me, to know she's safe.

"Do you have any word of home?" I ask her

quietly.

"Not since I was taken in by the Guild. You?"

"Haven't been anywhere but inside that castle for sixteen years up until a few days ago. No way to know." I close my eyes and hold her closer. "One thing I must tell you is how sorry I am that I couldn't come find you."

"You have nothing to be sorry about," Blaze insists. "I'm fine. We're still alive. We're together now. What more could we ask for?"

She puts her arm around me, hugging me close to her as I watch the fire. Belle and Horatius fall silent too. All of us are just enjoying the quiet night around us.

The silence is shattered by Alder's heavy stomping as he returns to camp. "We should probably get some sleep," he says. "We need to start moving as close to dawn as we can manage."

Blaze stifles a yawn. "Suits me. I'm exhausted."

"You can sleep on my bedroll, just beside me," I tell her. "I have an extra blanket."

"Don't trust us with your sister?" Alder teases.

"I barely trust you with my horse," I retort, helping Blaze get to her feet.

Before I roll over for the night, I cast a glance back at Belle. Seeing her beautiful face silhouetted by the fire, it's difficult to realize how much things have changed. Not only our situation but also our feelings for her.

There was a time when I burned with unparalleled hatred toward her for what she did to us. After some time passed, I merely resented her. Now, I can barely remember those harsh feelings I harbored towards her. All I can see now is the beautiful soul she is. A selfless woman who does all she can to make things better for the people who need her. The last reason for holding a grudge against her is gone with the return of my sister, even though we have a new complication, since Blaze is also one of the ten Chosen.

Indeed, our situation is so surreal I can't decide if I'm more astonished by my sister being one of the Chosen or the fondness I feel for my former tormentor—also a Chosen one.

As those thoughts pass through my mind, I say, "Goodnight, Belle."

She smiles and replies, "Goodnight, Beacon," before giving me a heartfelt smile. For just a moment, all is right in the universe.

Chapter Thirteen
Belle

I awaken in the morning to find Blaze and Beacon already up, stoking the dying fire and making coffee and breakfast (a few rabbits either Blaze or Beacon caught before we all woke up) for all of us.

When I ask why Blaze doesn't just conjure up a bigger fire, she ducks her head and looks a bit sheepish. I assume she's thinking of how she nearly incinerated herself and Alder to death yesterday, so I let the matter go.

Soon enough, Horatius and Alder emerge from their slumber and neither wastes any time packing up our gear so we can start traveling again as soon as everyone has a quick bite. While packing up, they become intrigued by something pertaining to the tents which causes Beacon to go over to join them, leaving me alone with Blaze for the first time.

In between sips of coffee, I ask her, "So what were you doing out there in the forest?"

"My job," Blaze replies, her unblinking eyes staring into the forest beyond. "I intercepted a message addressed to Kronos on my last excursion."

"What kind of message?" I ask, genuinely curious.

"A message asking Vita to arrive soon. When she does, it will spell doom for Delerood."

"When is she coming?" I ask.

"I don't know. All the message said was that she'd be arriving this month as discussed with Kronos."

"We have to get there first, prepare for her arrival," I tell her and she nods.

"For all the good it's done me so far," she scoffs, shaking her head. "Yesterday was irrefutable proof that I still can't control my powers. I'm not even sure what *I can do*."

"Many of the Chosen didn't always know they had the powers they do," I point out.

She nods, but doesn't seem convinced. "If I can't defend myself from a measly pack of hellhounds, what hope do I have against Morningstar?"

On one hand, I'm glad to hear Delerood still resists the enemy. Conversely, I fear for the lives of those who continue to fight. "Sooner or later, Kronos will realize his message never arrived."

"We have to get to Delerood before Vita arrives," I say.

Blaze nods, but there's doubt in her expression. "But how can we make it into the city?"

Beacon strokes his chin with his free hand. "I might know a way to do that…" Then he looks at me. "Have you ever heard of a *Long Winter's Nap*?"

"Are you fucking kidding me?" Alder replies sarcastically before plopping down to eat his own rapidly cooling breakfast. If the temperature of the coffee or food bothers him, he doesn't show it.

"Beacon doesn't kid about anything," Horatius comments before taking his first bite of breakfast.

"Oh, let me," Blaze says, rising to her feet. She walks in front of Alder and puts her open palm underneath his coffee mug. A slight sizzle and some steam rise from the coffee inside, making Alder's eyebrows shoot up in surprise.

"I thought you said you couldn't control your power," he points out.

"There's a big difference between warming up a cup of coffee and burning down your enemies," Blaze explains with a shrug. "The more heat I emit, the less control I have of it."

Alder looks down at his food and grunts. "Can you do that with my breakfast, too?"

Blaze smiles and holds out her hand. "Hand me your plate and find out."

"Could I be second in line?" Horatius asks, and Blaze turns to give him a quick nod and smile.

I ask Beacon, "So what is a *Long Winter's Nap*, exactly?"

"A hibernation spell," Horatius explains.

"Anyone enchanted by it appears dead."

Despite the heat Blaze creates, I feel a chill down my back that has nothing to do with the extinguished fire. "And how long does this death nap last, exactly?"

"Only until I decide it's time to end it," Horatius says with a shrug, putting his plate in front of Blaze. He takes a big sniff of the warmed food before holding out his coffee cup to her, to which she quickly warms the liquid inside up.

"This little death nap would give us a perfect introduction to Morningstar," Beacon says as Blaze finishes heating Horatius's coffee.

"How is that?" I ask.

He nods as he faces me. "We can say that your death broke the curse, and now we wish to rejoin Kronos's army once more."

"I would be the one to fake my own death?" I ask, clearly uncomfortable with the idea.

"You would be the only one whose death would interest Kronos," Beacon points out.

"Well, he might be interested in mine, as well," Blaze offers.

"Not like he would Belle's," Horatius responds and the others agree. I have to agree with him too—I've been a thorn in his side.

"I'm not sure I like that plan," Horatius says. "For one thing, how would we have even come across Belle's dead body… after sixteen years?"

"She came to Castle Chimera," Alder answers.

"That part can simply remain the truth."

"And what would be her reason for coming back after sixteen years?" Horatius asks, shaking his head.

"Simple," Alder says on a shrug. "We say we don't know," he continues between bites. "In fact, I plan to say I got so fucking angry at her turning up, I killed her on sight."

"You really are so much more than just a pretty face," Blaze teases as she walks by him.

Alder guffaws, but says nothing. He's too busy trying to clean the rabbit meat from the bone.

"I don't know," Horatius says, shaking his head.

"What if you can't break the spell in time?" I ask, keeping everyone focused on the topic. "You'll need my power to deal with Kronos, nevermind Vita."

"As I hope I demonstrated yesterday, and proved to your satisfaction, Belle," Horatius says after gulping the last of his coffee, "my powers are nothing to scoff at—even if I'm not convinced this plan is the best one—my powers shouldn't be the concern."

I remember his impressive presentation, yet I'm still compelled to say, "However, you're still honing those powers."

He shakes his head. "I'm merely reorienting myself with them. By the time we reach Delerood, I'll be more than ready to challenge my father." I hear the undertone of anger in his voice that speaks volumes. He fully intends to make Kronos pay for his past sins and transgressions. I'm just grateful it doesn't seem like Horatius hates me any longer. Actually, it doesn't seem like any of them do— well, Alder is still a touchy subject. Hate me? No, but there's still a certain animosity that hasn't dissipated.

"There's one other problem," Blaze interjects as she carries her dirty mug, walking to the pail of washing water. "No one said anything about locating Kronos. Do we even know exactly where he is? Where are we planning to go first? We might want to agree on that before we charge in with weapons and magic blazing."

"Before that happens, you should know that Kronos intends to use any opportunity to end my life," I add. "I dispatched many of his men before my people finally retreated from Delerood. Long story short, he wants to see me dead."

"A *Long Winter's Nap* would, no doubt, convince him you were," Beacon suggests.

"And what would stop anyone from driving a sword into her heart just for the sheer pleasure of doing so?" Horatius asks

"We would stop anyone who tried, of course," Alder says with fierce conviction. His stern expression is shared by Beacon.

"Stop him and you'd be killed for treason and they'd still insist on killing me, anyway. Do you see the problem there?" I ask.

"I see it," Blaze says, nodding.

The reasons I dislike the plan are purely personal. And I trust Horatius and Beacon when it comes to protecting me—they've already proven themselves. Alder doesn't feel obligated to protect me, true, but something in him has changed, as well. The old Alder would never have given chase when I was abducted by Gatz. His attitude towards me is definitely different from the time when I first released him from the spell but there's still something there—something angry and something untrustworthy. Furthermore, there's nothing I can offer or give him that I haven't already.

"I must agree we need to iron out the details," Beacon says, finishing off his breakfast. "But is there a better plan?"

"Maybe by the time we get to Delerood," I reply before putting my plate and mug in the washing pail. "I think I can devise something better than falling into a pseudo coma."

Horatius shrugs. "Certainly no harm in considering more than one option," he sagely says before handing his dishes to Beacon, who piles them atop his plate.

"You're going to make someone a fine wife and mother someday," Alder jokes to Beacon before handing over his used dishes.

"If you were half as funny as you are ugly, I might propose to *you!*" Beacon shoots back with a smirk.

"You could do so much worse," Alder counters.

"I can't possibly see how," Blaze quips as she helps her brother wash the soiled mugs, plates, and forks.

Alder laughs before taking a healthy swig from his flask, which he bought at our last stop. The alcoholic fumes emanating from it tell me the liquid inside certainly isn't water.

"Cocktails at breakfast?" I ask.

"Does Milady disapprove?" he asks with his usual amused leer.

"Reckless indifference, considering what's ahead of us."

"Ah, I'm a better fighter with a bit of drink in my gut on a bad day than most sober warriors are on their best day."

"I can vouch for that," Beacon chirps while Blaze plunges her hands into the washing pail. The water gently steams while she wipes the food off with a dish rag.

"Why, thank you, wife," Alder replies to Beacon with a laugh.

"You're not welcome."

"Now that the two of you are virtually betrothed," Horatius says, spearing Beacon and Alder with an amused look, he rises to his feet. "I'll excuse myself to answer a call from nature."

I look up to see Alder facing me and there's a

strange expression on his face. I'm not sure what to make of it.

For a song, he'd give you up in a heartbeat, I think.

Chapter Fourteen
Alder
Two Days Later

We've been on the trail for days now.

In all that time, Belle's hardly spoken to me.

And I'm not sure what the reason is for her silence. It's as though a switch has flipped in her because there was a while there when she and I were... civil. Now, not so much. Now, all I get from her is icy silence.

Thinking perhaps I was making an issue where none truly exists, I've observed her and come to the conclusion that she has no problem talking to the others. But when it comes to me, she's anything but friendly. When we travel, she rides as far away from me as possible and only speaks to me in short, terse sentences.

We haven't had sex for days, although I've thought about it and her nonstop. Ever since that night when she crawled into my lap and rode me for her sheer pleasure, I've been unable to think of anything else.

Yet, why she's so short and curt with me now? I have no idea.

Furthermore, I don't know why her silence bothers me. Sure, I saved her hide from that bastard, Gatz, in the forest, but so what? I'd do the same for any soldier on the line despite our previous clashes. So, her avoidance of me shouldn't create any strife in my mind. But it does! It digs into my skin like a cluster of splinters I can't extract.

And there's only one way to drive those splinters away.

After we finish riding for the night, I decide to approach her about whatever the hell is bothering her.

As we set up camp, I notice a slight rain starting, which means we'll have to pitch our tents this night. Just as well, because I want a bit of alone time with my witch. Thus, I pitch my tent a bit further from the others. Not that I give a rat's ass about Horatius and Beacon overhearing the sounds I intend to make with Belle. But I'm thinking of Beacon's sister, Blaze. Beacon hasn't been the same since we found her, and he tries to protect his sister from every little thing. I nearly laugh at his incessant coddling, but I might rouse his anger if I have it out with Belle and Blaze finds the sounds… off-putting.

After everyone retires to their tents for the evening, I wait until the rhythm of snoring fills the air and then I start for Belle's tent. Though hardly as stealthy as a cutpurse, I do my best to sneak up on her. Once I'm close enough to stick my head inside her tent. I find her still awake.

"What do you want, Alder?" she hisses at me as soon as she sees me, and the venom in her tone is audible.

"I want to know what in the bloody hell is wrong with you," I tell her in a low a voice.

Her reaction is a disgusted snort from her nose. But I don't allow her response to throw me. Hate me she might, but desire me, she still does. I've seen the truth in her eyes—how she watches me when she doesn't know I'm looking.

"Tell me why you're really here," she says.

"Because I want from you the same thing you want from me."

She swallows hard, and I realize my words are true. She wants me just as badly as I want her and she can't deny it. Perhaps she won't even try.

"The others will overhear," she starts as I shake my head, a grin overtaking my mouth, because I realize I've got her exactly where I want her—she wants me inside her, and that's exactly where I want to be.

"That's why I set up my tent further from the others. Follow me?"

She stares at me for a few seconds before nodding and dropping her attention to her feet, as if she's angry with herself for giving in. I'm not certain why it is, but that knowledge causes my cock to stiffen all the more. She's fighting herself—that's how badly she wants me, how much I've gotten under her skin.

She obediently follows me out to my tent. As soon as we're inside and I've closed the fold, I turn to face her.

"Take your clothes off," I instruct. She obeys me instantly and once she's completely bare, I tell her to get down on all fours. She immediately drops to her hands and knees and arches her back in such a way that the whole of her is spread to me. I can scent her on the air and her desire is thick.

I pull my cock out from my trousers and leaning down, tease her opening with my head. As soon as I touch her, she arches and then pushes her hips back against me, as though trying to spear herself on me. In response, I push into her.

"Deeper," she begs me.

Burying myself as far as I can inside her, her pussy walls clench around me and it's all I can do to hold my orgasm in. She feels like heaven and it's been too long since I experienced her, so I'm overly eager. And apparently so is she, because after I thrust inside her another three times, her orgasm erupts around me.

I can't restrain myself a moment longer and I explode inside her. Our bodies collapse against one another before we land on the floor. She suddenly climbs on top of me and takes me into her strong but soft hands, stroking my burgeoning hardness.

When my staff reaches full mast again, she

straddles me, rising upward before she impales herself on my stiffness and begins a slow, methodical ride up and down my length. Her hips grind against mine, and I happily fill her up with every inch as her body moves provocatively and our eyes stay locked onto each other. Her moans become small cries, and I have to muffle a few of them with my palm. Offering her all of me, I relish the way she bites her lower lip as she indulges herself so uninhibitedly. Her hands press on my abdomen with all the weight she can put behind them.

"Oh, gods, I'm coming," she moans right before her body shudders. Her fingers dig into my abdomen, scoring fresh red welts before she collapses against me.

I seize the moment and flip her over, continuing to thrust into her. I'm slow and calculating, but soon I'm so close, I can no longer contain myself. I answer my own need and fill her with my seed.

Afterward, all I can do is lie back on the floor and stare up at the tent of the ceiling, listening to the pitter-patter of the rain.

It's another few seconds that I notice she won't look at me and barely reacts to me as she throws her clothing back on.

"I'm returning to my own tent now," she says, as though I've become an inconvenience she has to endure. I find her indifference insulting.

"No, you aren't."

She glares at me. "And why is that?"

"Because we aren't done." I point to a pile of blankets in the corner of the tent. "Sit down over there."

I watch her sit down on the pile. I have to admire her despite my anger and it takes everything I have to remain unmoved and not react to the sight of her sitting there with tight lips and her arms crossed against her buxom chest. I could take her again, and there's a part of me that desires doing just that, but I have something else that must take priority.

"All right, I'm sitting," she says. "Now what?"

"What is your problem with me?" I demand, narrowing my eyes at her. "I know we're not exactly friends, but I thought we developed a mutual respect for each other. All you've done since Blaze joined our party is avoid me like I'm a leper."

"Excuse me? I don't suppose you realize you just fucked me, so how am I ignoring you?"

"Never mind the sex."

"That would be a first," she mutters contemptuously, while avoiding my eyes.

"What's going on with you?" I demand. "With us?"

"Since when does hate-fucking include pleasant conversation?"

I inhale deeply. "Is that what you think this is?

149

Hate fucking?"

"Isn't it?"

I swallow hard because, no, it's not what it is, but I'm not sure I want to admit as much to her. She doesn't budge but looks at me as if there's a detail she missed. Then she surprises me by saying, "You still hate me."

"Is that what you think?" I ask, genuinely surprised.

"That's what I *know*," she corrects me. "I haven't survived this long without learning to read people. I'm quite sure that if you believed it necessary, you'd offer me to the enemy without a second thought."

I shake my head. "You really believe that of me?"

Once more, she fearlessly gets in my face. "Give me one reason why I shouldn't."

I slowly exhale out of my nose. Anger doesn't scare her any more than violence does. The only way to reach her is by telling her the truth. "I don't deny a small part of me still hates you for what you did to us, *to me*." I glare at her. "But I fully understand now why you did what you did."

"And yet you still hate me."

"I tend to hold grudges, sure," I answer on a shrug. "Usually against people who dare to cross me in some way. If I didn't, I'd probably be dead and buried a long time ago." I blink and seriously consider my next words. I don't want to admit it, but the truth must be the *whole* truth. "Besides, the passion between us doesn't lie. There's something much stronger than hatred here."

"Fucking isn't a gesture of affection," she sneers.

"Agreed, but not all men are the same," I argue. "Some men prefer to give their ladies roses and jewelry. I like to fuck you until you can't possibly come one more time."

"How romantic!"

My eyes harden. "Don't try and pretend you don't like it." I take a breath. "And, in case you've forgotten, I'm also the kind of man who would make Gatz regret the very idea of *ever* coming after you again."

She studies me and some of the anger leaks out of her gaze. "Are you trying to tell me you… actually care about me?"

I breathe in deeply. This isn't easy for me. "Would it be so terrible if I did?"

"No," she answers quickly and drops her attention to her fidgeting hands. "I just… didn't think you did."

"The fact that I did what I did about Gatz should tell you how much I care and… how devoted I am to you." I take another breath. "If I didn't care about you, I wouldn't have gone after him."

She doesn't say anything, but looks down at the blankets beneath her. I wonder what she's thinking. She studies my face as if trying to decide if I'm telling her the truth.

"I know our... association is a bizarre one and it might have started with hate-fucking, but that's not what it is now... for me, anyway. I hope it's not just hate-fucking for you," I offer.

She looks at me for a few seconds. "It's not that for me either." She affectionately pushes a hand across my jaw. "And I'm sorry I wasn't... very kind to you recently."

"Apology accepted."

She sighs and leans against me. "You are a tough man to understand."

I chuckle as I push her long hair behind one of her ears. "I believe I'm fairly easy to understand."

As we lie there, I can feel myself growing thick and hard again. Whenever I'm around this woman, she stokes my passion like no one does.

"You're hard again?" she asks on a laugh.

"You bring the beast out of me," I answer as I reach down and start rubbing her between her legs. Even though she wears her pants, I can feel the heat of her sex beneath them. I lean forward and kiss her, happily expressing the passion I feel for her.

Truth be told, there's much more on my mind that I want to say to her, but I can't find the words. Perhaps I don't need words at all. Maybe I've already conveyed my thoughts with my actions.

Still, I hope to find the right words to tell her

how I feel some day. Not today. Right now, I need to be inside her because, for some strange reason, she feels like home.

Chapter Fifteen
Horatius

The closer we get to Delerood, the less I like
Beacon's plan.

Couple that with my lack of enthusiasm for
returning to Delerood in general and my mood
turns considerably sour. I wind up riding silently
beside the others as we reach the outskirts of our
destination. They barely seem to notice. Beacon is
constantly conversing with Blaze, while Belle and
Alder chat softly in ways they foolishly think no
one will pay any attention to.

That leaves me alone with my thoughts, which
I find poor company indeed. For the thousandth
time, I rack my brains to devise a better way to get
close to Kronos, and ultimately, Morningstar. No
new insights or workable notions come, however.
Strangely enough, I erroneously imagined I would
have more time to find such a way. Now our time
is nearly run out. All we have is Beacon's original
plan, one that doesn't thrill me.

My mental conflict ebbs and surges inside my
head when we stop at a pub to rest, dine and
retrieve whatever supplies we can get. Three strong

ales fail to improve my mood, so I excuse myself from the table and step outside. While inhaling my first deep breath of fresh air, I hear the sound of footsteps behind me and then I feel a hand on my arm. I turn to see it belongs to Belle.

"What's on your mind, Horatius?" she asks, pulling me sideways to face her. The dimming dusk only enhances her lovely face.

"Nothing of any importance," I lie. "Just mentally rehearsing the plan and trying to think of what, if anything, we still need to do."

Her furrowed brow speaks volumes. I clear my throat and add, "It's nothing to concern yourself with."

"I'm about to put my life in your hands!!" Belle counters, shaking her head as she scoffs at me, "so I beg to differ. Now, tell me what's bothering you?"

Naturally, she deserves to know, but I hold back, because I don't want to add concerns to what must already be a load of worry on her shoulders.

"Look," she finally says, placing her hand in mine, "I can tell something is bothering you and I care about you, Horatius… I want you to tell me."

I squeeze my hand around hers. "And I care about you too. Therein lies the problem."

She looks curiously at me and I realize there's no turning back now. "Kronos has already taken everything I ever cared about," I explain. "I can't let him take you too."

"If we do this right, he won't," she whispers and gives me a full smile.

But my anxiety isn't eased by her words. "Doing it right is the part I'm worried about. I'm not sure I can play my part in front of the Kronos with the level of persuasion it will require. Not when I detest him as much as I do."

"And why shouldn't Kronos believe you? There's no reason for him not to believe you killed me, thus breaking the curse that kept you trapped! He'll most likely welcome you as a hero."

After a few deep breaths, I conclude, "Then let us hope Kronos never glimpses the truth in my eyes as clearly as you do."

"Oh, Horatius," she says, "I know he's done nothing but torment you and I know how you feel about him—I hate him too. But you're different now. You're better than he is. Kronos can never hurt you or anyone you love again."

I look towards the ground. "I hope you're right."

She smiles up at me and moves a step closer. "I *know* I'm right."

I nod before the two of us just stand there, staring into each other's eyes. She takes another step towards me and I lean down, wrapping my arms around her as I kiss her softly. She returns the kiss with fervor and I'm not sure how long it is that we stand out there.

"Are you… are you and Alder… together?" I

ask her at last, wanting and needing to understand the nature of their relationship because my feelings for her are genuine.

She breathes in deeply. "That is a subject I don't really know how to answer," she says.

"I understand that, but I have... feelings for you, Belle," I respond. "But I don't know if I can or should act on them if Alder is in the picture."

She smiles up at me. "I have feelings for you too and while Alder is in the picture, I'm not sure to what extent." She breathes in deeply. "I don't know... what I am to him. Whether he cares or if I just happen to be the flavor of the month."

"What is he to you?"

She hesitates. "I care about him."

I nod and don't push her for more, because I see the predicament she's in and I don't believe there will be any easy answers. Instead, I follow her back into the pub.

Alder spots us first and waves towards the steaming plates of roast lamb awaiting us.

"Good timing!" he calls out before tipping back a fat tankard of ale. I find myself growing more and more irritated with the man because I doubt whether or not he realizes how lucky he is to have the favor of such a wonderful woman. Alder always has been a bit of a womanizer and I don't doubt he's changed his ways. I can only hope so, for Belle's sake.

"Take it easy on that stuff," Belle admonishes

him. "You can't be skunked when we ride into Delerood."

Alder gives her a dismissive laugh. "As though one pint of ale will cause me to be hammered!"

Despite his joviality, the rest of us seem a bit subdued while we eat our meals. Not necessarily a bad thing, I suppose, since the time has come for everyone to focus upon our mission. The moment we step through the gates of Delerood, we must be ready for anything. And getting through the time-loop Kronos weaved won't be an issue because his blood pumps within my veins, thus the timeloop will recognize me and allow me to pass through.

We finish our food quickly and pay our tab. When we step outside again, Belle and Alder head to the local chemist, just two shops over. Meanwhile, my eyes land on a nearby fruit stand. Or rather, on the sizable wagon that sits beside it. The storage compartment I spot underneath it solves a problem I've yet to resolve until this very moment.

The boy minding the stand looks at us with suspicious eyes as we approach. "Fair evening, young master," I greet him.

"Save it, mister," the boy replies in a harsh tone that his high-pitched voice betrays. "You here to buy something or what?"

I gesture towards the wagon. "No, I wish to borrow your transportation."

The boy crosses his arms. "It ain't available."

"We only require it for one evening, *this* evening. Afterwards, we will gladly return it to you."

"Long before that, my pa will skin my hide for coming home without it," he retorts, shaking his head adamantly.

Blaze appears at the front of the wagon suddenly and asks, "Is that a pomegranate?"

"Aye, I've just got the one left," he replies as he lifts it up.

Blaze's face splits into a ready smile. "How much for all the fruit that's left?"

"All the fruit?" the boy asks, frowning to show his confusion because it's fairly obvious she won't be able to eat it all. "You're kidding, right?" the boy replies, his vain attempts to appear older are belied by his youthful inexperience and undeniable surprise.

"I never kid about business," Blaze tells him, "and if you loan us your wagon, we'll buy out all your stock."

I give Beacon a look that tacitly inquires, "is this a good idea?" He waves me off and pats his purse with confidence. Meanwhile, the boy is obviously torn by our generous offer.

"You promise you'll have me cart back here by mornin'?" he finally asks as Blaze and I nod in unison. "I'll tell Pa you needed it to get all the fruit home."

Blaze takes one of her hands off the

pomegranate. "Then it's a deal?"

The boy readily takes her hand and shakes it. "It's a deal, Milady."

Five minutes later, we hitch up the horses and pull away with the cart. The boy distributes the fruit we paid for to an eager throng of young children who appear to be hungry and all of them wave their thanks to us. Belle and Alder join us, carrying a vial with the *Long Winter's Nap* potion they got from the chemist.

Alder nods his approval at our new transportation as he and Belle climb into the back. "This should do the job."

"One can only hope," I mutter while eyeing the potion in Belle's hands. "Are we certain the chemist did exactly what—"

"He's an old friend," Belle assures me. "And one who knows his business."

As we pull into a quiet alleyway, I bite my tongue and hope with all my heart she's right. I just—if anything happens to her, I don't know how I'll ever forgive myself.

Once we come to a halt, I ask Belle, "Are you ready?" Alder takes the role of sentry to be sure no one enters the alley while we prepare.

"As ready as I'll ever be," Belle answers, handing Beacon the potion. While Alder guards the alley, Belle lies down and crosses her arms over her chest. Beacon and Blaze sit down on either side of her.

"See you soon," Beacon tells her as he ministers the few drops of potion necessary. It seems as soon as Belle swallows the draught, her eyes slam shut and her breathing becomes so shallow, it's hardly detectable. A moment later, she has no pulse, no heartbeat, and no breath.

"She looks… dead," I say, frowning. "Very persuasively dead."

"She isn't dead," Beacon answers, "just sleeping. No different than the locket's effect and just as quickly reversible."

His obvious attempts to comfort me clash with what I see before me.

"I can still hear her breathing," Blaze says. "Her heartbeat too. Both of them are slow. But they're still there."

Alder gives her a nod and looks down at Belle with what appears to be concern in his eyes— concern and something else—love? I can't imagine how that would be the case, given the fact that this is Alder, but perhaps… perhaps he's changed?

"Well, let's get going, then," he says. "Our old commander won't kill himself."

"How much easier that would make our task," I mutter.

Beacon reaches for his sister. "This is where you get tucked into the hidden storage compartment of the wagon."

Beacon helps her climb into the open hatch before closing it along with our spare weapons.

Now, the Chosen One in our party appears to be dead while the other hides inside a concealed wooden box. My urgent desire to settle my nerves is paramount when Alder turns the wagon towards the fortress of Kronos.

Beacon and I sit in the rear, flanking Belle. My heart pounds with panic as I look at her still form. Beacon's eyes drift elsewhere a few times, but always come to settle on the storage compartment where his sister hides.

Alder comes to a halt before the heavy iron gates and the blast of energy which surrounds them—the time loop. I step forward and hold my hands up to the forcefield and it instantly rescinds, just as I knew it would.

The battlements above the gates are manned by young soldiers who would have been no more than children when we first disappeared.

"What business have you here?" one of them asks in a gruff voice.

"That's between us and our mutual commander, pup," Alder retorts.

"I know every soldier under Lord Kronos's banner, graybeard," the soldier spits angrily. "I'd certainly recognize your face if you'd shown it before now."

"We were cursed by a witch for sixteen years, so I'd be very surprised if you ever saw my face, stripling," Alder snarls.

"Bit late getting back here, Grandfather," the

soldier snaps and I watch Alder's eyes narrow. Truly, we aren't much older than they are.

"True enough, but back we are," Beacon says. He gestures to Belle's supine form and adds, "And we brought the witch that cursed us to boot. She'll be worth something to Lord Kronos."

The guard squints as he looks inside the wagon. Turning back to us, he asks, "What are you called?"

"Beacon."

"Horatius," I chime in, figuring it's no use to tell them I'm the son of Kronos because they probably won't believe me—I'm more than sure it's believed I'm dead.

"Your papa, for all you know," Alder quips and the guard frowns at him as Alder raises his brows and gives the man a charming smile. "But Prince Alder to anyone else." He swivels his head to the back. "And she was known as Belle Tenebris... when she breathed."

"And what makes you think Lord Kronos will want to see you?" the guard asks warily, clearly not recognizing Belle's name. He doesn't dare turn us away but remains leery of us, as he should be.

Suddenly, I grow weary of his tedious protocol. "Stop wasting our time! Inform his lordship that his son has finally returned!" I say, figuring the time to rely on my blood relation is now.

"Horatius?" a familiar voice says from behind

the guard. The face of an old soldier appears although I fail to recall his name after all this time.

I wait until he gives all of us the once-over. Then he smiles. "Always knew you'd survived somehow." He motions to his fellow guards. "Let 'em in. Lord Kronos will want to see them post-haste!"

I nod my appreciation when the heavy gates slowly creak open. My heart thuds loudly against my chest as we roll the wagon through. The thought of facing my father again is bad enough, but the notion of lying to him is terrifying.

Chapter Sixteen
Alder

Even before we reach the Kronos' current residence— the palace of Delcrood—I can feel his presence.

The hairs on my arms and the back of my neck rise on their own. The echoes of our footsteps cease for a moment and I look around myself, noticing that every candle sconce on the wall is free from any wax sliding down their tapers. When the doors to the hall finally open, I'm instantly reminded why I feared this bastard so long ago.

"Horatius, my son!" Kronos calls out from the back of the hall, his arms spread wide. "I can hardly believe you're back." Kronos' voice resonates with the same strange echo I heard from our footsteps. I take in his chest-length beard in shades of gray and black and see that he's aging quickly.

"Neither can I, Father," Horatius replies, walking over to return his father's embrace. I admire his self-control and I know that however much I detest Kronos, Horatius hates him even

more. Yet, he smiles in his role as the dutiful son. I
doubt I could resist the urge to shove a blade deep
into Kronos's gut the moment I got close enough.

After their hug ends, Kronos finally
acknowledges my presence. "Your Grace... or
should I say, 'Your *Disgrace*'?"

"My Lord," I reply politely, clenching my
teeth. I hope we can pull this stunt off and make
Kronos believe all of us are still as loyal to him as
ever because I want nothing more than to see him
dying at the end of my blade.

"Now then," Kronos says, turning his eyes
back to Horatius. "I understand you return to me
with a gift."

"I do," Horatius answers with a clipped nod.
"We have brought you the witch who cursed us
more than sixteen years ago."

"Can it be?" Kronos asks, his eyes narrowing
on Horatius.

Horatius nods. "She's a Chosen One!"

Kronos's eyebrows shoot up in happy
astonishment. "Have you any idea which one she
is?"

"Belle Tenebris." Again, my admiration for
Horatius's acting is unparalleled.

"Ah, she is one of the most powerful," Kronos
says on a nod. "Lord Morningstar will be quite
pleased to hear this," he continues, clapping
Horatius on the shoulders with both hands. "She
caused us quite a bit of trouble."

Horatius gestures towards the rest of the hall. "Seeing how firmly in control our forces seem to be, I'd imagine not *too* much trouble."

Kronos chuckles. "Yes, well, the good news is: the witch will trouble us no more."

Kronos looks over at me, and I see a strange smile on his face. I meet his gaze without flinching. Just when I have to blink, he nods and asks, "Well, where is she? I would very much like to see this dead Chosen One."

I indicate down the hallway. "She's still laid out in the wagon. Beacon is watching her."

"Watching her? Do what? Decompose?" Kronos asks with a skeptical chuckle. "If she's truly dead, she hardly needs a guard, does she?"

"With all due respect, Father," Horatius says, "a Chosen One is no mere person. They possess extraordinary powers. We dare not risk the chance of anything happening to her body before we can seal it inside one of your display cases."

A light of understanding dawns in Kronos's dead, dark eyes. "Yes! She will become a permanent reminder to the populace and the resistance of the perils they face if they dare defy us. What better example to discourage them than a Chosen One? A *dead* Chosen One?"

"Be sure to add how our slain witch kept the three of us cursed in isolation for sixteen years as monstrous beasts before we slew her," I add, throwing all the heat of my hatred for Kronos into my words. "It makes the example ever more threatening."

Kronos bellows out a raucous laugh. The ugly reverberations down the hall make my skin crawl. Is it due to the broken enchantment or just the realization of the horrible tyrant I was so blindly serving?

"Of course," he says as his laughter dies. "You shall prove to be a fine ruler, Horatius," Kronos says as he returns his gaze to his son while pacing the hall, his usual habit when he's in deep thought. "Very well, we shall keep her in the glass case while we await the arrival of our reinforcements."

"Reinforcements?" Horatius asks, pretending to show surprise. "Are things not as well under control as I assumed?"

"Oh, they are, indeed they are," Kronos replies. "But Vita is soon to arrive."

I'm relieved to know she hasn't arrived yet.

"Now, then, Alder," Kronos says, looking into my face. "Do make yourself and Beacon useful by fetching our deceased guest and sealing her inside the provided case."

"At once, My Lord," I say, gritting my teeth as I pound my chest in a primal salute. It's close to my usual manner, so he takes no notice. I'm almost relieved when I head out the door and distance myself from him—just so I can breathe.

When I leave, I hear him telling Horatius, "I believe this homecoming calls for a grand celebration. Lord Morningstar will be very interested to hear the details of how you and your comrades dispatched the witch."

"Would you like to hear the details first?" I hear Horatius reply as I round the corner. I pray the story he weaves is a convincing one. For all I know, our true intentions are already as clear as day.

Beacon and I return to the hall, carrying Belle inside the large glass display case.

"Excellent," Kronos says as soon as his eyes land on her and he claps his hands together jubilantly. Pointing towards the center of the room, he says, "Over there, if you will." He and Horatius speak in hushed tones as we maneuver the case into position. After we finish, Kronos saunters over to get a better look at Belle.

"Diabolical, yes, but utterly beautiful," he remarks, studying her as if she were a famous statue. "I can only hope at least one of you had a romp with her before she died," he says on a chuckle as he turns to face me, clearly knowing my reputation with women.

Beacon and I exchange a secret look. I'm clenching my fists tightly to resist the urge to strike him down for that gratuitous insult—to Belle.

He hums and says, "Pity she's no longer alive or I would test her out myself." He strokes his chin.

Fighting the impulse to punch him right in his repulsive mouth, I notice Beacon is having just as much trouble as I am from the look of pure hatred on his face. Fortunately, Kronos isn't facing him or me.

"Well, I imagine you are eager to shake the dust of the trail off your boots," Kronos says with another thunderous clap on Horatius' back. "You have my leave to do so. But after that is accomplished, do return here."

We chorus another round of assurances, promising we will, and the guards guide us to our rooms. I hate the idea of leaving Belle alone but there is nothing I can do.

The sound of people's happy voices flood our ears long before we reach the dining hall.

The raucous crowd we see when we enter reveals the success of the celebration. Servants circulate among the guests and soldiers, bringing trays of hors d'oeuvres and liquor to launch the festivities.

In the center lies Belle, thankfully unmolested and undisturbed in her glass showcase. It's almost unbearable for me to see her like this. She looks dead and although it's only a disguise, it still tears my heart right out of my chest. She'd be surprised to know that, given my previous behavior towards her. But the animosity I once felt toward her is tempered now by my gratitude. And my concern for her continues to grow. I don't pretend to understand how this can be, only that it is.

Gods strike anyone who dares to harm her…

Meanwhile, Horatius spots Kronos and catches up to ask him, "Should we not wait for Vita before beginning our meal?"

"I believe Vita is currently detained in the city on business. Once that is resolved, she shall join us."

"Detained with… pockets of resistance?" I blurt out.

Kronos gives me a peculiar look. "And if there are?"

Knowing I might have blundered a secret, I quickly cover up my mistake by adding, "I'm just sorry I can't assist her in their eradication."

That wry smile curls Kronos's lips. "Not a day has passed since your return and you're already so eager to fight for our cause."

"In all the time I've known him, My Lord," Beacon interjects, "I've never seen Alder any other way." He takes a breath. "And this cause is all of ours," he adds. "Sixteen years in captivity has only strengthened our resolve to see the rebels put down."

Kronos nods towards my comrade. "I can understand that. A great deal of pain to be compensated, am I right?"

"More than I can describe," I truthfully tell him.

"I'll admit there remain some stubborn factions," Kronos says, linking his arms behind his back. "Delerood is completely under our control. More than half the citizens either fled or met their demise. The rest are imprisoned." Another look of amusement appears on his face. "I expect most of them will make excellent hellhounds."

Beacon and I both have the good sense to remain silent.

"I do recall Lord Morningstar's intention to locate Bastion and Andric from our previous conversation," Kronos adds. "They turn out to be surprisingly slippery enemies to corner."

"Perhaps I could find them," I volunteer, thinking this would be an absolute opportunity to win them to our side. I've no doubt they still command a legion of their own men—men we could use in our attack against Kronos. Yes, this is most fortuitous—if it comes to be.

Kronos eyes me with a mix of curiosity and amusement. "You are very eager to return to your duty."

"I'm eager to be on the move after being cooped up in that castle for more than sixteen years, My Lord," I clarify.

He scrutinizes me. "And why do you think you will succeed where my other soldiers have failed?"

I do not flinch or falter under his intense gaze. All I have to do is tell the truth. "Because for hunting down my lordship's enemies, there is no one better than I." I take a deep breath. "Some things never change."

An insincere smile splits his lips. "Considering how a single Chosen One managed to bring down the three of you, I beg to differ."

I'm unconvincing. I must think of something else to say and quick. "True, she caught us with our pants down," I admit, "but as my Lord Kronos concedes, she was no ordinary witch. And the curse left me with an interesting benefit."

In the blink of an eye, I shift to my chimera form, ripping my clothes to rags and prompting more than a few revelers to back away from me in fear. I take a moment to savor their terror before Kronos says, "This is your cursed form?"

"Yes! And now I can shift any time," I reply through my lion mouth. "And also locate Lord Morningstar's enemies once I have their scent!"

My demonstration over, I revert back to my human form. The ladies stare at the glorious endowment between my legs but I ignore their awe. The only person I wish to share it with now is sealed up in that damned showcase.

Kronos claps his hands for a servant. "Get something to cover His Grace's dignity!" Then he

173

turns his attention to me. "Consider me convinced, Alder. Though I hate to cut your festivities short, I'm afraid we will need you to embark upon your excursion shortly as the hunting party's ship is due to pull out from the harbor within the hour."

"Very good, sir," I answer, realizing with a jolt that there's no way I can back out of this now. Regardless, finding Bastion and Andric is exactly what I need to do—in order to bolster our own side. Yes, the timing of this journey is quite good.

The servants return with a change of clothing which they hand me.

"Let us not speak of any more business for now," Kronos proclaims, clapping his hands once more as he faces the room around him. "Let the celebration begin!" Then he faces me once more. "Good luck out there on the waves, Alder. I look forward to your return."

Chapter Sixteen
Belle

I'm in a strange place, caught between not quite life and not quite death.

I'm in an odd, halfway place that could only exist in the infinite depths of the soul. There are moments when I feel like I can climb to the surface. Then I'm dragged down into the ceaseless, chaotic fever dreams. I keep skipping from one to the next, so often I fear I may go mad. But in the all-too-brief moments of clarity—near wakefulness, even—I can hear the voices of those around me. They sound as though they're miles and miles away, but I know they're here—around me. I can almost make out some of the words when the latest fever dream strikes me down.

I'm sitting at a small table.

A wooden cutting board with slices of bread and a thick slab of butter are between my father and me. A jar of fresh strawberry jam is on the left side. Sun shines through the windows behind us and my sister pours a glass of fresh orange juice. From where I'm sitting, I can see the orange tree growing outside our home, the source of the sweet juice. As the memories return, they just as quickly vanish, along with the food and drink on the table. Then everything else disappears.

The three of us now face each another with anguished expressions. My father furtively peeks down the hallway as if he senses something lurking there. Unsurprisingly, he speaks to us in a soft tone, lest we are overheard.

"I'm so sorry I can't be there to help you."

"I'll be fine, Father, no matter how it turns out," I reassure him, doing my best to convince myself to believe my own words.

He gives me a brave smile. "I know you'll fight valiantly. You always do, and you always have." The smile dims a little as he adds, "But the time will come when your fight must end. Don't fear the day when it comes."

"You mean if *it comes," I say with false bravado. "Don't underestimate my abilities so quickly. Don't forget, I've got people whom I can rely on. People who will see me through."*

"So, you do," my father replies, looking reassured. "Still, this is not such a horrible place to dwell. While you are away, we shall make this as much your home as it is ours. We will all celebrate your return. But please, Belle," he puts his hands on my shoulders, "above all else, there is so much more to life than this incessant fighting."

"This fight has been going on forever already," my sister adds, leaning forward to help herself to a crust of bread. As she slathers it with the fresh butter and takes a bite, it suddenly dawns on me that the food is back. When I reach for the bread, however, it vanishes from sight once more. My sister ignores it, smiling happily as she chews her buttered crust.

"Seems that way, sister," I admit, *"but I hope we end it soon."* Turning to my father, I add, *"And if I must sacrifice my life for that to happen, so be it."*

"I know," he replies softly. *"But as your father I pray and wish you survive this war."*

The moment he finishes speaking, he and my sister vanish. The table is empty and bare again, with not even a crumb left behind. The sunny view outside the window is suddenly obscured by darkness. As I look around at what was my home only a moment ago, I find nothing but black walls, ravaged by time and fire. The roof above me is gone, giving me a grand view of the night sky. The glowing stars and full moon are a cruel mockery as I stand in the burnt remnants of my childhood.

The head of a crook suddenly appears in the chair opposite me.

"Things always look more promising in the daylight," the crook's owner says.

Even though I can't see the face of the newest guest, the crook in her hand is a dead giveaway. "Bowie," I breathe.

"Belle," she says as though we just ran into each other on the street instead of in this phantom location.

"Have I passed to the other side?" I ask. Bowie's a shepherdess that guides the newly deceased to their afterlives. So, her presence might well mean that.

"Not yet," she says in a reassuring tone. "You're currently suspended between life and death."

Her words fill me with dread. "Am I going to die?"

"Oh, eventually, of course you are. We all do. It's inevitable."

"You know that's not what I mean," I tell her impatiently. "Am I going to die here and now? Before I even have a chance to participate in the final battle?"

"As if I could tell you that," Bowie says with a roll of her eyes. "My role is to simply show the souls where to go after they pass over. How they got here in the first place is another matter entirely."

"Why are you here then?"

She shrugs. "This is your dream, why don't you tell me?"

I contemplate her reply for a moment, doing my best to reason things through. "I doubt I will ever emerge from the Long Winter's Nap. I believe I'll die."

"Just remember the prophecy, Belle," *she says, rising from the table.* "And your part in it."

As she fades back into the darkness, I hear her quote the appropriate passage:

"Distant wrongdoing demands a toll
And a sorceress will pay the fine
And rising from contrition
Shall stop the march of time."

She quickly dissolves into a gray mist. Moments later, the charred remains around me likewise begin to fade, leaving only a vacant, black nothingness.

Then I hear voices nearby, growing louder as my surroundings begin to fill with light. I find myself sitting at the head of a table. On the opposite end sits Kronos, surrounded by his underlings. Despite my presence, none of them seem to notice me.

"The problem, friends, is that Morningstar wants it all," *Kronos explains to his entourage.* "He wishes to take over the entire world to punish the one that rejected him."

"Surely you understand why he would do so, Lord Kronos," *one of the men says.*

"Understand? Of course, I understand!" *Kronos replies with audible irritation.* "But my *sympathy wanes dramatically when the end result is indentured servitude for all of us."*

"For all his power, Morningstar cannot run this world by himself," a second underling scoffs. "Surely, we too would have a place of importance in his new order."

Kronos's eyes glower with disdain. "If you believe that, Lineaus, you are much more naive than I ever estimated. Morningstar's loyalty begins and ends with himself."

"Even so, My Lord, what other choice do we have?" a third man opines. "We either go along with his plan or become casualties with everyone else. He has no shortage of lieutenants who would prefer the first option."

"Would it not be better to be the leader than the led?" Kronos asks as the others frown their confusion.

Kronos chuckles as he continues, "We shall do exactly as Morningstar says. But only until he achieves his final victory. Then, once he feels triumphant and comfortable, we depose him! And we take his empire as our own."

"How can we accomplish that?" Lineaus asks.

"The finer details still need to be worked out, but…" Kronos stops speaking as the sound of approaching boots echoes across the tile.

"We shall speak more of this later," Kronos whispers just before the owner of the heavy boots appears. I can't glimpse the newcomer from my

vantage point, but Kronos happily confirms her identity. "Vita! Have your troops finally arrived then?"

I try to make sense of what I just witnessed. It isn't like all the fever dreams. What is the significance of what I saw?

I must confess a new epiphany in my journey of self-discovery. I have an entirely new appreciation for Horatius, Alder and Beacon. Being trapped for sixteen years in the bodies of beasts must have felt like an eternity. My own "curse" has a much shorter duration, mere hours, yet it's already unbearable. I realize all at once their collective hatred of me was justified. I hope I get the chance to tell them how sorry I am before this is over.

Chapter Seventeen
Beacon

"Beacon, is that you?" I hear a woman ask.

Turning toward the sound of her voice, I'm surprised to see a face I've not laid eyes on in years. "Desdemona!" I exclaim, even though the surprise isn't exactly a good one. All the while, I note how much she's aged since last I saw her. While still a very beautiful woman, the wrinkles on her face reveal the harsh passage of time.

"When I heard you'd returned, I had to see for myself," she purrs, running a hand along my shoulder seductively. "In fact, the last time I saw you, you were wearing far less clothing than you have on now."

"So I was," I reply, doing my best to recall the last time we met. Subconsciously I feel the need to take a step back from her but I refrain.

"I was certain you perished in the fighting," she says, continuing her gentle stroking. "And I was devastated by the news. Yet here you are, exceeding everyone's expectations, and going even further in your successful career by retrieving the corpse of that awful hag-witch that kept you from us all those years."

I don't like her reference to Belle as a *hag witch*, but I don't dare tip my hand. "Here is a far better place than where I was."

Desdemona aims one of her practiced smiles at me before joining the depraved standing near Belle's glass case. "I have to confess, even in death, she remains very beautiful."

"As it stands, I do wish Kronos would order her body to be burned just like the trash it is."

The question now becomes how I could ever have bedded someone so inhumane as Desdemona?

"I believe the glass case is a good place for her to be," I answer, subduing my anger.

"You always were such a gentleman," she says. "Well, most of the time anyway!" She giggles before adding, "Anyway, I suppose it doesn't matter. If I know Kronos, he'll most likely keep her as his trophy, or a deterrent to the populace, or both. I would have thrown her worthless corpse to the hellhounds and been done with it."

I have to clench my teeth to resist the urge to launch into a tirade. Belle is a much better woman and person in general than Desdemona, who is no more than a high society whore, who swapped her soul to Kronos for his protection. Since then, she's laid with most of his army, ever hoping to find someone dumb enough to marry her. Alder, of all people, was the first to point out her depravity. My own judgment was rather flawed in those days. Horatius also figured her out before I did.

The three of us often shared women—far too many to count—but our trysts were always consensual. Desdemona was the only one who ever attempted to use us for something other than sex.

Even Belle didn't go to such lengths. She offered herself to us as recompense and atonement. Belle had no ulterior motives. I respect people who state their clear intentions. By contrast, I disrespect any woman like Desdemona.

A snap of her fingers jolts me from my distant thoughts. "Beacon, are you even listening to me?"

Suddenly, I can't stand another moment near her. "Enjoy the party, Desdemona. I must be going now."

"Going? Where?" she sneers.

"Anywhere but here," I reply, walking rapidly away from her.

"Rude!" I hear her hiss behind me, but I barely pay her any attention. There's something in the air that doesn't seem quite right. It's not just because we're surrounded by the enemy, although that certainly puts all of us on edge. And we're one man down with Alder's absence. But I can't shake the feeling that something ominous is afoot.

We have to get Belle out of that case—I fear—and soon.

Inexplicably, my thoughts suddenly concern the future. If we escape this horrible place, I'll ask

Belle to stay with me—with us, if the others agree to it. Why? Because the truth of the matter is that even though I've never so much as kissed her, she touches me in a way no other woman ever could. My feelings for her are precious and I wish to continue experiencing them, however long that may be. I know now, beyond all doubt, that Belle must be in my future. I'm just as certain the lonely Horatius and brutal Alder might share my future plans with her. I've no qualms about that possibility if it manifests. What greater peace can there be than to share the woman of my dreams with my two closest friends, the men I value most?

I hear loud footsteps approaching.

Looking up, I see Kronos and a small group of his men talking near where Belle lays. Approaching them is another group of men. I quickly step behind a throng of people, attempting to get lost in the audience. A hush falls over the gathered party goers, but then their voices rise again in a chorus of whispers and hushed conversation. The new group winds its way through the center of the crowd toward the great hall. As they get closer, the crowd draws back to allow them passage.

Over the five or six heads before me, I spot Vita with her retinue now moving behind her, allowing her to take the lead rather than surrounding her protectively. She approaches Kronos with a sickening smile and extended hand, offered in greeting. He walks toward her, obviously eager for her arrival. I watch him wave toward Belle's display and she glances in that direction, nodding appreciatively before he directs her toward his private chambers nearby for whatever discussions they intend to have out of public view.

Her men follow. No doubt they'll stand guard outside. As they pass, I spot Gatz in their midst. He stops as he sees Belle in the glass case beside him and studies her pointedly, clearly wondering how in the world she ended up here.

My stomach drops.

"How did she get here?" he asks loudly.

Kronos stops for a moment and turns back to face him. "She was brought in by soldiers I thought I'd lost decades ago, including my own son. It was quite the pleasant surprise. I was just telling Vita that I've saved Belle Tenebris for her enjoyment— a very special delight to welcome her."

Gatz shows no sense of pleasantries as he begins to sweep the room with his gaze. I duck behind the man in front of me, not at all eager for Gatz to spot me.

"Soldiers?" Gatz repeats, eyes narrowing. "What are their names?"

I freeze as he locks eyes with mine, just as Kronos gives him our names. "My son, Horatius and his fellow soldiers, Beacon and Alder. They are here somewhere. Did you already know of my returning heroes?"

"They aren't heroes," Gatz spits the words in response. "They're traitors!" Then he turns to face me once more, taking a step nearer. "Isn't that right, Beacon?"

I look around, finding no sign of Horatius. Looks like I'm in this one alone. Thus, I lunge sideways and grab the sword of a nearby guard, squaring off against Gatz. "I am no traitor," I lie.

I'm grossly outnumbered, even if Horatius comes to my aid.

"Still an aspiring rapist, Gatz?" I challenge him, hoping this accusation might paint my fight with Gatz about something other than a betrayal of Kronos.

"I will no longer be 'aspiring' as soon as I've dispatched you. I trust the fair Belle isn't past her expiration date… as you've led Kronos to believe."

I rush him, hopeful I can shut his mouth before he says too much. Somehow, I need to repaint this narrative, make it seem as though Gatz is the one who should be worthy of suspicion, not myself.

He dodges and continues to spill my secrets for all to hear as our swords clash against one another amid the guests, some who have shrunk away from the fight while others wait for a command to join in.

"This man is plotting against you, my lord," Gatz says as he glances at Kronos.

"Guards, take Beacon into custody," Kronos roars, but his words are cut off as Horatius appears from nowhere and joins the fight.

Alder

It feels good to be on the open ocean again, even under the given circumstances.

As Kronos said, the ship embarking in search of Bastion and Andric left as soon as I arrived. It was a small ship with perhaps four or five men on board. But, truly, it would take no more than that to apprehend only two men.

Kronos had written a command that said the previous captain was relieved of his station and I was to take over and that missive was delivered by Kronos' personal messenger. Though the man was irritated to be reprieved of his duty, he left the ship all the same.

Now, four hours later, I find myself just off the shore of Cassion Island, where it's believed Andric and Bastion are located. After dropping anchor, I order the men to depart the ship and we trudge through the sea water as we approach the sand. I instruct them to spread out and look for Bastion and Andric in different directions, as a plan takes shape in my mind.

There is little hope of taking all five of these men on together, but they're no match for my prowess with a sword. Yes, I consider allowing the chimera to take over, but the truth of the matter is that I want to give these men a fair fight, but one on one.

As they separate, I make my way to each of them, one by one, and launch my attack. They each put up a good fight, but I'm successful in every challenge, just as I knew I would be, and I easily pick them off one by one until I am the only one left standing.

As I now focus on my task at hand—locating Andric and Bastion, I notice signs of inhabitation—footprints in the sand, piles of refuse. Yes, I'd bet my life on the fact that both of them are here.

As I travel further into the center of the island, surrounded by exotic trees and underbrush I don't recognize, I pick up on the scent of something roasting over a fire. Pushing through the growth, I emerge on the other side of the island and instantly recognize the two men where they stand, just off the shore, talking with a red-headed woman.

This must be their bride, Aria.

I'm very close to them, much closer than they realize.

As I take another step forward, I watch Aria hold up her hand up as though to quiet them. She turns then and looks directly at me as I step out from the shadow of the trees behind me.

"I'm not here as your enemy," I shout, holding up my hands in supplication.

"Prince Alder," Andric says, his eyes

narrowing as he recognizes me. "Who is loyal to Kronos and Vita."

I shake my head and Aria glares at me. "What are you here for?" she demands, facing me as rage travels through her eyes.

"I am no longer in league with Kronos, Vita or Morningstar," I answer, keeping my hands up high. "I've come here because I need your help. *Belle Tenebris* needs your help."

"Belle? What have you done to Belle?" Aria demands, moving closer to me in a menacing manner.

"I've done nothing to Belle. In fact, I'm here on her behalf. We both need your help."

"Help with what?" Bastion asks, wearing a replica of Aria's suspicious expression. Not that I blame them—I understand how this must look but I'm determined for them to see the truth, no matter what. I can only hope they'll willingly travel back to Delerood with me.

"We must overthrow Kronos and Vita."

"I don't believe you," Aria says and shakes her head. "Belle would never come to you for help," she continues to protest and to glare at me. "Belle hated you enough to curse you all those years ago."

"Sixteen, to be exact," I answer. "Look, I know this is hard to, believe but it's the truth. At this exact moment, Belle is lying in a glass case in the center of Kronos' new home which he's set up in what was once your palace in Delerood."

"Is she… dead?" Aria asks, her eyebrows knitting in the middle of her face.

I shake my head. "She's under the influence of *Long Winter's Nap*, but she's in the middle of the lion's den, along with my friends, Horatius and Beacon. All three of them are in trouble."

I begin to tell them everything that's happened from the point at which Belle arrived at Castle Chimera.

"And Belle is now laying in a glass display case like some sort of museum piece?" Aria asks, horrified by that portion of my story. "What if they kill her?"

"Horatius is there to protect her."

"What if something happens to him?" Aria asks, shaking her head. "This sounds like an incredibly stupid plan."

"I can't argue that, but it was the only way we could get inside the palace and find out what Kronos was up to so we could prepare to end his reign of terror."

"We must leave here at once," Aria announces, standing up and retreating from the fire where it looks like they were roasting a small boar.

"I have a ship," I answer. "It's small enough that the four of us can adequately sail it."

"We can be in Delerood in three hours at most," Andric says as he stands up.

Chapter Eighteen
Horatius

Kronos bears down on me, although I'm already on my knees in the center of his ballroom. I've already been attacked and I've suffered a blow to my side, which is now bleeding down my waist and staining the entirety of my left side.

"How could you have deceived me like this? My own son!"

"Son? How dare you even use that word to describe me." I spit the words back at him. "You're only my father because you raped my mother and put me in her belly."

A large grin overtakes his hideous face as he nods. "Just as your mother meant nothing to me, neither do you. As of this moment, you are dead to me, Horatius. I'm going to destroy you, but first, you'll watch me destroy your precious Chosen whore."

He pulls away, turning toward Belle, where she lies in her glass case. He seizes the doors and rips them open, throwing them on the ground where they break into thousands of pieces. But Kronos is unconcerned as he pulls her from inside and drops her to the floor. Then he begins dragging her across the floor, not concerned as she paves the way through the glass shards, before turning to face me.

"Bring him," he barks back at his men.

His men haul me to my feet, even as I can barely walk—I've lost too much blood and I feel beyond weak.

"Sit him down there. I want him to watch this as he takes his last breath," Kronos says.

I try to struggle as they force me into a chair and hold me down. I'm too weak to fight them.

Opposite me, Kronos orders Belle to be held in place by a man on either side of her. She's still lost to the power of the potion she drank and, thus, she's powerless. Kronos reaches forward and gripping her blouse, rips it in two, following with her breeches. Then he leers at her naked form and his men do the same.

"How was it, son?" Kronos asks as he turns to face me. "Did you enjoy trading your birthright for this?" He motions to her. "There must be something special between her legs," he growls, reaching out to put his hand between her thighs.

"Don't you touch her!" I roar at him, trying to fight against those who hold me down, but it's no good.

"The witch certainly captured you with her sex…"

"I never… *experienced* her." I spit the words at him. "So, no, you've got that all wrong, *father*."

Kronos throws his head back and laughs before he settles his expression on me once more. "Then you are a bigger fool than I imagined."

I watch, in horror, as he motions to one of his men who hands him a whip. Then he steps up to Belle and begins lashing at her upper body, leaving deep gashes behind on her back, her arms and her breasts.

When he finally stops, I'm beyond relieved she's still under the spell of the *Long Winter's Night*. Hopefully, she can't feel anything that's happening to her.

"Hmm, it seems that potion was most effective," Kronos comments as he turns to face me and a cunning expression overcomes his face. "So, my son, you protect this witch and yet, you've never known her intimately?"

"That's what I said."

He nods and then motions for his men to pull me up to my feet.

"Then you're going to know her now, so you can experience exactly what wasn't worth you becoming a traitor to your own blood."

"What... what are you saying?" I demand, worried as the weight of his words sinks into my mind. He can't mean...

He laughs again. "You're going to fuck her in front of us all."

I swallow hard, even though I'm not sure if he's saying this just in jest? Could this simply be a

sick joke, something meant to humiliate me? Or
does he actually intend for me to do this? In front
of his soldiers? I can only hope not. And not so
much for my own sake, but for Belle's.

"And when you are finished," he continues. "It
will be my turn." He looks over to his men. "We'll
keep her in the family." His men scoff at his joke
and he faces me again. The men who were
previously holding me down, lift me to my feet and
force me forward.

"I don't have the strength left to even stand
up," I argue, shaking my head. "Let alone… what
you're ordering."

Kronos nods and then approaches me, placing
a hand on my shoulder. Instantly, I feel my strength
returning and as I glance down at the wound in my
side, I realize it's no longer there. He's healed me
simply so he can humiliate me. And, I've no doubt,
he plans to kill me afterwards. But not before
adequately torturing me—such is his way.

The men on either side of Belle drop her, and I
reach out to grab her before she lands on the
ground.

"Take her now," Kronos says.

I look at him. "And if I refuse?"

"Then I will order Ramkin, right there, to slit
her throat," he answers and motions to his man,
who pulls out a sword and holds it close to her.

"Okay," I say simply as I breathe in deeply and
then focus on Belle's face. Yes, I've thought of this

moment many times—wanted it many times—but I never thought it would happen like this.

As I lower her to the ground as carefully as I can, I reach down and begin stroking her face, trying to get her to wake up. I can't do this to her if she's unconscious—it's just too wrong on every level. Even now, it's beyond wrong, but I have no choice. And, unfortunately, neither does she.

"Belle," I whisper into her ear as I pull my fingers across her cheeks. "I need you to wake up."

Even though the potion is potent, my magic should get through to her—should rouse her. And seconds later, I see her eyelashes begin to flutter as her lips move as though she's whispering something to me. I swallow hard as I allow my fingers to travel from her cheeks, down the line of her neck and her collarbone and further south—to her breasts. I run my fingers across her nipples and, in response, they pebble.

"Wake up," I whisper again and hold one of her nipples in my fingers, squeezing it slightly as the bud hardens even more. Her breathing hitches and I imagine this must be another sign that I'm getting through to her.

"Belle," I whisper again, into her ear, so no one can hear me. "I need you to wade through the shadows and come back to me," I say as I trail my fingers down her body until I find the junction of her thighs. When I run my finger past her hard and sensitive nub, her body shifts beneath me.

"I'm not interested in you warming her up," Kronos spits at me.

I glance up at him and feel my eyebrows meeting in the center of my forehead. "Either I do this my way, or I don't do it at all."

He says nothing more and I return my attention to Belle. I shift my fingers down further, fingering her opening, which grows wetter as I run my finger across her slit, without entering her.

"Belle," I whisper again.

This time, her eyes pop open and she immediately focuses on me, a look of confusion registering in her eyes. It's then that I realize I don't want her to know she has an audience, and an audience with Kronos, no less. So as she holds my gaze, I weave a charm—disallowing her to see or focus on anything but the two of us. I imagine the room around us empty and as she takes stock of her surroundings and doesn't seem concerned, I realize my magic has done its job.

"Horatius?" she asks hesitantly. "Where… where are we?"

"I need you to focus on me," I say as I smile down at her, wanting to make this as easy on her as I can. "I want you to feel me and enjoy what I'm doing to you—it's just us and we have this moment… I want us to take it."

It's then that she realizes my fingers are on her most private of places. I lean down and claim her lips, and she opens her mouth to me. As soon as her tongue meets mine, I push my index finger inside her and she bucks beneath me.

"Tell me this is okay," I say as I pull away from her and stare into her eyes. "Tell me you're okay with this and that you want it… that you want me."

"Of course," she says on a nod and smiles up at me. "You know how I feel about you."

"And you know how I feel about you," I respond, almost forgetting the fact that a group of men is witnessing this.

I push another finger inside her, and she arches beneath me. "That's it," I coo at her and begin pushing my fingers in fully before pulling them out again. She's beyond wet and so tight, I'm not sure I'd be able to get another finger inside her.

She moans out and instinctively opens her legs to me and I reach down to toy with the buttons on my trousers. "Do you want me inside you?" I ask. I need to hear her tell me this is okay because my guilt is fully flowing within me. I need to understand she wants this as much as I do, even if the circumstances are so wrong.

"I've always wanted you," she whispers.

It's enough, and I free my cock from my breeches as I spread her legs further to make room for myself. Then I feed the head of my cock into her opening as she arches underneath me and moans out her need. I push inside of her and she feels so good, I almost forget the circumstances.

I push all the way until I'm seated fully inside her and she wraps her arms around me as I pull out and thrust back in again. Our bodies fit together as if they were designed for each other.

"Yes, yes, yes," she calls out, her nails digging into my back as our rhythm increases.

I can feel her muscles contract around me, bringing her ever closer to an orgasm. She takes me along with her, and I'm so close, but I hold back. I want this to last. I wish I could stay inside her forever, but that's an impossibility

Truly, it's hard to believe this is happening.

It's another second or so before I burst within her and she relaxes against me, smiling up at me as she trails a hand through my hair.

"Take him to my chambers," Kronos interrupts and the power of my spell that kept her from realizing the reality of the situation washes away in a spike of fear as she realizes where we are.

Belle

I don't understand what's happening or how it's possible that Horatius just made love to me, and now I find myself in a room with Kronos and his goons. But I have little time to figure that out

199

because before I know what's happening, a thunderous noise from the opposite side of the room grabs my attention.

As Horatius is being pulled away from me and I search for something with which to clothe myself, an enormous cyclops enters the room. It's Beacon in his cursed form and he's so immense, he has to stoop to fit in the room. One of the guards jumps up and threatens Beacon with his sword, but Beacon simply grips the sword and throws the man into the wall so hard, his neck snaps.

As another man approaches him, I watch Horatius free himself from the men leading him from the room as he suddenly reaches down to scoop up the fallen man's sword. He immediately runs one of the men through with it as Beacon dispatches the other. Horatius faces his father then and motions for him to come closer.

Kronos laughs in his face. "You're not strong enough to combat me, son. You never have been."

"I'm not your son!" Horatius roars at him.

But Kronos makes no move to attack. Instead, he simply stands there, wearing a grin as if he knows something Horatius doesn't. As I watch them, no longer concerned with my nudity, I watch Horatius who suddenly drops the sword and then falls to his knees as he cradles his head between his hands and an expression of ardent pain overcomes his features.

"Can you feel me driving into your brain,

weakening you as I push further and further, threatening to drive you over the edge into a madness you won't be able to escape?" Kronos asks on a laugh.

"Stop it!" I scream at him and as he turns to face me, he simply holds his arm upright and I feel a burst of energy seize me around my middle, launching me backwards, into the wall.

"I can feel the hopelessness seeping inward, threatening to drown your will," Kronos continues as he faces Horatius again. "You're slipping away, being consumed by me as I worm deeper and deeper until you can no longer hold me back."

Horatius collapses to the floor in defeat, Kronos driving his attack into Horatius' mind like a dagger's blade. I stand up and taking a deep breath, close my eyes as I try to pull my magic to the forefront but I'm shocked when I realize my magic is nowhere to be found. Pulling on it again, there's still nothing.

I can do nothing but watch as Beacon approaches Kronos from behind, holding a large spindle from the side of our wagon. As Kronos turns to face him, he drives the spindle dead center into Kronos' right eye. The latter drops down to his knees as he screams his agony and Beacon reaches down, pulling Horatius to his feet.

Horatius immediately turns to face me and runs towards me as I close the gap between us. He grips me around the waist and the three of us rush from the room.

"Here," Beacon calls out in the baritone of the cyclops (at least, I think that's what he says) as he throws a drape he apparently pulled off one of the windows at me. I grab it and pull it around myself, trying with difficulty to keep it wrapped around my bleeding and naked body on our way out to the wagon.

I don't understand why but my back is stinging as though I've been stabbed. And as I look down at myself, I can see welts all over my chest that must have been brought on by a whip. It's then that I realize Kronos must have whipped me while I was under the power of the potion.

Even though Kronos was just skewered by Beacon, his power is still great. And mine is diminished, owing to my own wounds and the fact that the *Long Winter's Nap* isn't fully out of my system—at least I think that's why I was unable to call on it earlier.

As soon as we enter the ballroom, I notice people scurrying this way and that, owing no doubt to Beacon's arrival as Cyclops. As we turn the corner in our attempt to flee, we run headlong into Alder. Behind him are faces I haven't seen in too long: Aria, Bastion and Andric.

"We have to act quickly," I tell them. "I can't do much right now, not physically, but my mind is still stronger than Kronos anticipated."

"I can help," Aria says with a curt nod.

"Is it mostly Kronos' men in Delerood?" I ask. She nods. "Almost entirely."

I follow her onto the balcony that overlooks the city and the sea. Then I breathe in deeply and imagine casting a wide net over the city, ensnaring every last soldier loyal to Kronos. Then I turn to face Aria, watching as she slowly raises her hands into the air and calls to the waters of the ocean that surround us. As she calls on her magic, it almost feels as though her magic reaches out to me, calls upon my own, because I can suddenly feel a tingling I couldn't before. As I stand there and open myself to the ethers, I feel Aria's magic helping to fill up my reserves and then I release my magical net.

A roar fills our ears as the water rises from the depths and approaches the shores. As we stand there, she hits the city with a huge wave, washing as many of the unprotected people, Kronos' people, out into the sea as possible. The waves simply part around each of us, keeping us safe even though we stand in the center of it. Meanwhile, those around us are picked up by the waves and pushed out to the sea. Wails and screams surround us, only to become gobbled up by the roar of the water.

With one massive tidal blast, our enemies are sent screaming into the dark depths of the surrounding waters, dragged back to the pits of the ocean from which she commanded the water to do her bidding.

"Now, Blaze!" Aria shouts, dropping her hands so that the water settles back into place. Not even realizing Blaze is present, I turn to face her and watch as she reaches down and hits the water with a burst of fire, causing the water to boil for those caught in it who haven't already drowned.

I watch as Kronos and Vita stumble out toward the shore just as the water erupts into a bubbling hot spring and sprays steam all along the shore. They're caught in it as they realize too late what's happened.

"We should go after them," Alder barks. "I want to rip them limb from limb."

"No. There isn't time for that right now," I say, shaking my head as I reach out and grip his arm, just to make sure he doesn't get any stupid ideas. "We have to heal and get our strength back. We're not fit to take them on right now."

I look at Horatius then as he looks back at me—a silent understanding passing between the two of us. We're the only two capable of dealing with Kronos and Vita directly and even as I turn my head back to them, they're no longer there— it's as if the air swallowed them whole.

"Well, I guess they live to fight another day then," Alder growls, clearly angry.

Chapter Nineteen
Beacon

Horatius manages to heal his wounds and uses what's left within his healing crystal to heal the wounds Kronos left on Belle.

After the altercation with Kronos and Vita, we are understandably exhausted but opt to stay the evening in an inn just beyond the borders of Delerood. Come the morning, we will start our journey home, where we plan our next strategy in order to overcome Morningstar for good. For now, we need to rest.

As Horatius heals Belle, Alder and I sit outside the small room, seemingly for an eternity, waiting for them to emerge, each of us quiet as we sit with our own thoughts. Aria and her two husbands have been busy trying to deal with the damage of Delerood and Blaze offered her help in doing whatever they require of her. She's meant to meet up with us soon.

"Horatius had sex with Belle," I say as I turn to face Alder, not sure why exactly it occurs to me to tell him this now, but it does.

He nods and doesn't appear very surprised.

"When?"

"Kronos forced him to… in order to humiliate him, I believe." I take a deep breath. "But she was a willing participant."

Alder nods again, before turning to face me. "Why are you telling me this?"

"Because I think it's important you understand how he feels about her, how *I* feel about her."

"And how is that?"

"We both love her, Alder, just as you do."

Alder nods again and grows quiet and I wonder at his thoughts. There's no expression on his face, so his mood is impossible to read.

"And what of Belle?" he asks finally. "Does she return your feelings?"

"I believe she does," I answer on an inhale. "But I mean to find out." Then I grow quiet for a few seconds before I face him again. "I know you have something between the two of you… but are you willing to share her?"

"If that's what she wants," he answers immediately and then looks over at me, nodding. "Then yes."

When Horatius and Belle finally step outside, looking none the worse for wear as they approach us, both of them seem to be all smiles and their feelings for each other are as obvious as the sun in the sky.

"Feel better?" I ask as I look on Belle's flawless skin and smile at her.

"I do."

"Can we talk for a moment?" I ask as I face Horatius and Alder and both nod at me.

"Sure," Belle answers, giving me an expression of curiosity. "Is everything okay?"

"Yes," I answer and then take a deep breath as I try to figure out the right words. "I've come to realize that… I have feelings for you, Belle." I pause. "We all do."

"Are you asking me to choose among you?" she asks, looking concerned.

"We're asking you to tell us what you want," Alder answers.

She swallows hard and looks at each of us in turn. "I love… all of you, but I feel as if I'm wrong in admitting that."

"You aren't wrong," I say, and the others nod their agreement.

"And if that's your choice, that's your choice," Horatius adds.

"You mean…" Belle starts, but then tears fill her eyes and she can't seem to finish her statement. I pull her into my arms and kiss her. She places her hands on either side of my face and returns my kiss eagerly before pulling away and smiling thoughtfully up at me. It's the first time I've ever experienced anything intimate with her and it's everything I hoped it would be.

Moving away, she kisses Horatius and Alder in the same way, looking from one of us to the next, as if she isn't sure where to start. I decide to help her, moving in to begin undressing her as Horatius moves behind her, kissing her neck and shoulders as I strip away her clothes.

"Of the three of us," Alder starts as he faces me. "You're the only one who hasn't yet experienced her," he says. "Perhaps you should have this moment alone? Just the two of you?"

I shake my head. "I can think of no better way to express my love for this incredible woman than to do so with the both of you. I want you here."

They both nod and then I turn to face Belle. "If that's okay with you, of course."

She beams up at me. "It's more than okay. It's perfect."

Then I hold her in my arms, kissing her softly as I lay her down upon the bed and Horatius spreads her legs and begins pleasuring her with his tongue. She moans all the while and the sound of her pleasure is the most incredible thing I've ever witnessed.

"She's ready for you, Beacon," Horatius says.

I shake my head. "I want to watch you take her."

He doesn't argue but steadies himself at her opening and when he enters her, he drops his head back as he shuts his eyes and Belle moans out as she arches her back. Horatius takes his time with her, pushing in and out of her until he finds his rhythm.

Alder takes my place and holds her in his arms. She beckons me closer as Horatius finishes inside her, pulling out and revealing how wet she is. She invites me to kiss her nipples and express my own love for her. I sit down beside her then pull her atop me and instruct her take what she wants. Her lithe body slips up and down the length of my cock, her tight center milking me for everything I have to offer.

I can't express how beautiful she is as she rises and falls on top of me. She's like an angel as she takes her pleasure from each of us, showing off her perfect form as we share our love for her in the only way we really know how. Words can be exchanged, gifts can be given, but the ultimate expression of love is found in the passion of skin on skin, soul to soul.

Her body shudders as she orgasms, enjoying our lovemaking in a way that makes it obvious how much we mean to each other. I let loose my own orgasm and kiss her once more, before giving her over to Alder.

As I watch them, I'm surprised at how gentle he is with her. We've shared many women, but I've always known him to be rough—though not with Belle. With her, he's obviously enamored in a way I've never seen him behave with another woman.

There is nothing here but love. Love between one woman and her three men, men who will always be there for her and protect her as best as any man can protect a woman.

At least the three of us would. Always and forever.

Belle

"They proposed?" Blaze asks, all smiles.

"Yes." I say, smiling at the memory. In fact, all it seems I've been doing lately is smiling.

Blaze lights up, clearly happy at the news and it feels good to tell someone.

"When is the big day?"

"We haven't set a date yet. We agreed to wait until the war is over," I take a deep breath then and the unsaid words "*if we even survive the war*" hang in the air. But I immediately put the thought out of my head. I'm too happy to focus on my own worry.

"We have so much to do still," I continue. "There's no time to focus on a wedding."

"I know how happy you make Beacon and the others, of course—but especially my brother. He's finally in a good place these days, and that's all thanks to you."

"Well, it's also thanks to getting you back into his life," I add. "He makes me happy, too. They all do." I breathe in deeply as the real reason I sought her out returns to me. "But, Blaze, I need to discuss something with you right now."

"Oh? What's on your mind?"

"While I was under the effects of the *Long Winter Nap* potion, I had periods of lucidity when I could hear what was going on around me. And I heard Kronos talking with Vita about how he plans to overthrow Morningstar after the war is over."

"Well, that's good then, isn't it?" Blaze asks, appearing confused by my expression of concern. "I mean, it's good that they could potentially be fighting each other."

"Yes, but… I wonder if we could use that information to help us before it ever gets to a battle between them."

"How do you mean?"

"I believe we should alert Morningstar to Kronos' deceit."

Blaze's eyes go wide. "What will telling Morningstar accomplish?"

"It will weaken their bond," I answer as she begins to nod, seeing the beauty in my plan.

"How would we even get this information to Morningstar?"

I nod, figuring this would be her next question. "If you can get an anonymous message to Morningstar, one that can't be traced back to us, a message that reports that Kronos plans to double cross him—it will sow seeds of distrust between them."

"But why is it a secret?"

"The less who know, the better. If the message

is a secret, it reduces the chances of it getting tracked back to us."

She nods again. "I can deliver it in secret."

"I'd like for you to go tonight, if that's okay?" I ask as I breathe in deeply. "The sooner we get a bee in Morningstar's bonnet, which will, in turn, stir up trouble in their ranks, the better."

"Yes, tonight is fine."

"We need to buy ourselves time to move forward with the plans we're laying out to defeat them, but we don't want them to have the same luxury," I continue. "If we can get them to do some of the dirty work against themselves, then we're already ahead of the game."

"I'll get going immediately," Blaze says and appears eager with her new job. "Just let me go tell Beacon that I have to go on a mission, and I'll be on my way."

Epilogue
Blaze

I made sure Belle's message is delivered to Morningstar by intercepting one of his soldiers and pretending to be a spy within Kronos' ranks. The soldier eagerly took off with the message and before he could question me, I snuck back into the darkness of the forest.

I streak away as quickly as possible, hoping to get away as cleanly as I arrived, but it's too much to hope for. I'm barely outside the edge of Morningstar's camp when I begin to smell the all too familiar smell of hot sulfur.

I can't see perfectly, but I can still make out the hazy forms of hellhounds who are now hot on my trail, pursuing me and as they grow closer. I can tell by their particular smell that they're the same three I've been trying to elude for weeks.

I hurry, putting as much ground between us as possible, but the beasts remain in hot pursuit, no matter how fast I move.

To Be Continued in…
BLAZE

Get FREE E-Books!

It's as easy as:

1. Go to my website: www.hpmallory.com
2. Sign up in the pop-up box or on the link at the top of the home page
3. Check your email!

About the Author:

HP Mallory is a New York Times and USA Today Bestselling author who started as a self-published author.

She lives in Southern California with her son and a cranky cat, where she's at work on her next book.

Printed in Great Britain
by Amazon